GREATER THAN RUBIES

Book 2 of The Jewel Series
by

HALLEE BRIDGEMAN

Published by
Olivia Kimbrell Press™

Olivia Kimbrell Press™

COPYRIGHT NOTICE

PUBLISHED BY: Olivia Kimbrell Press™*, P.O. Box 470, Fort Knox, KY 40121-0470.

The *Olivia Kimbrell Press*™ colophon and open book logo are trademarks of Olivia Kimbrell Press™.

*Olivia Kimbrell Press™ is a publisher offering true to life, meaningful fiction from a Christian worldview intended to uplift the heart and engage the mind.

Some scripture quotations courtesy of the King James Version of the Holy Bible.

Some scripture quotations courtesy of the New King James Version of the Holy Bible, Copyright © 1979, 1980, 1982 by Thomas-Nelson, Inc. Used by permission. All rights reserved.

Original cover art by Amanda Gail Smith (www.amandagailstudios.com).

Library Cataloging Data

Names: Bridgeman, Hallee (Hallee Bridgeman) 1972-

Title: Greater Than Rubies; The Jewel Series book 2 / Hallee Bridgeman

　240 p. 5 in. × 8 in. (12.70 cm × 20.32 cm)

Description: Olivia Kimbrell Press™ digital eBook edition | Olivia Kimbrell Press™ Trade paperback edition | Kentucky: Olivia Kimbrell Press™, 2012.

Summary:Robin Bartlett said, "Yes!" Will she say, "I do," when the big day arrives?

Identifiers: ePCN: 2017900482 | ISBN-13: 978-1-68190-047-6 (trade) | 978-1-68190-048-3 (POD) | 978-1-68190-075-9 (hardcover) | 978-1-68190-049-0 (ebk.)

1. Christian romance fiction 2. man-woman relationships 3. suspenseful love stories 4. sisters family saga 5. sisterhood relationships 6. redemption faith grace 7. marriage holy matrimony

　PS3568.B7534 G743 2012 [Fic.] 813.6 (DDC 23)

GREATER THAN RUBIES

Book 2 of The Jewel Series
by
HALLEE BRIDGEMAN

Greater Than Rubies is a <u>Finalist</u> in the *Spiritual* category for the **2014 EPIC™ eBook Awards**.

DEDICATION

For Kaylee Anne...

At fifteen, my daughter, Kaylee, read *Sapphire Ice*, the first book in *The Jewel Trilogy*. She fell in love with the book. As she read, she would enthusiastically discuss the characters and what she thought about the story with me. I remember the evening she sat on the couch across from me finishing up the book on her Kindle. I knew she neared the end, and I felt excited anticipation at the prospect of discussing how it all resolved with her.

Suddenly, she sat up and said, "That's it?!"

I looked up and said, "What do you mean?"

"No wedding?" Kaylee waved her Kindle in the air. "You take me through all that and don't give me the wedding? I need the wedding, Mom."

So here it is, my darling daughter. This is my gift to you...

The wedding of Robin Bartlett and Antonio "Tony" Viscolli.

TABLE OF CONTENTS

PROLOGUE

Robin **Bartlett stood barefoot** on the white beach with water lapping at her ankles while her toes slowly sank into the sand. The sun beat down hot against her neck, and the wind blew her cotton skirt around her legs. She took the rubber band out of her braid and slowly loosened her long blonde hair, wanting to feel the strands blowing in the Florida breeze.

She felt Antonio "Tony" Viscolli approach before she heard him or saw him. Some radar inside of her perked up and she slowly turned, a smile on her face. The sun reflected off of his jet black hair, and she swore that his olive skin had darkened in just a few hours of sun and sand. He took off his sunglasses and she felt her breath catch at the look in his dark eyes.

Tony stopped in his stride and she could tell that he wanted to simply drink in the sight of her in such a rare happy, relaxed state. After a few heartbeats, her warm, welcoming smile and the sparkle in her sapphire blue eyes beckoned him closer.

"I can't believe that it's Christmas Eve," she said. She ran her hands along her bare arms. Bare arms—in December! "Do we even know what the weather report for Boston is today?"

The second he stood close enough to touch, his arm snaked around her waist. She loved the feel of him against her. "I don't check the weather there until I have to go back. And I typically avoid going back during the winter months."

Forgetting everything but the bliss surrounding her heart, Robin asked, "Why?"

Tony squeezed her close before releasing her. "I don't like to be cold." He gestured to the mammoth house behind him. "I'm like a bird. I fly south for the winter."

Robin heard a squealing sound of glee and shielded her eyes to look up at the house and see one of the adopted O'Farrell children diving off of the high dive into the pool. They had come to spend Christmas with Tony and, from what Robin could understand, they accompanied him every year. An older laugh chased the squeal, and Robin saw her sister, Maxine, go flying off of the high dive. Obviously, they were engaged in some sort of game of tag.

"It looks like you typically carry a flock with you."

Tony grinned. He turned back to look out over the aquamarine water that stretched out beyond his private beach in the Florida Keys. He pulled her closer so that she wrapped her arms around his waist and laid her head on his shoulder as they watched a sailboat meander along the horizon.

"Do you row here?" She knew he rowed on the river water in Boston as a way to relax.

"Only in my gym." He rested his head against hers and closed his eyes. "I windsurf here."

"That sounds like fun."

"I'll teach you how tomorrow." He squeezed her close then pulled away, running the tips of his fingers down her arm until their hands linked. "Want to take a walk?"

"Sure." She disengaged her feet from the sand and stepped in line with him. "I am so happy that you invited us here for Christmas. I love it here."

"I do, too." He gestured at the water. "God's design is so perfect. It humbles me when I come here. It's a place for me to come when I start feeling a little too full of myself, a little too big man on the campus. I come here and I look at this expanse and the gloriousness of perfection and remember that it's all God, and it's all about God."

She stopped and smiled at him. "I love listening to you, especially when you're talking about God."

He turned slightly so that he faced her. "What do you like about me speaking?"

Admiring him in his cotton pants and white cotton short sleeved shirt, his skin dark in the sun, his eyes a rich chocolate brown, she felt the rhythm of her heart speed up. She suddenly wanted to kiss him, to keep kissing him, to never have to stop. She felt her tongue dart out, lick suddenly dry lips, as those images started popping up in her mind. "Well," she said, stepping forward so that she could feel the heat of his body. "I love your voice. And I love your passion. And," she said, feeling bolder than she had ever felt in her entire life, she reached up and put her hands on his shoulders, "I love the love in your voice when you talk about God."

He put his hands on her hips. "You like my voice, *cara*?"

Grinning she leaned forward and ran her lips along his cheek, feeling for the first time ever, a day's growth of stubble. "Especially when you say words like *cara*."

"Oh?" His voice sounded suddenly thick. "You like Italian, eh?"

"Yes." She skimmed her lips over his cheek, down his chin, and along his other cheek. "Very much so."

He cupped her face in his hands and pulled her back just far enough to cover her lips with his own. He kissed her, drinking her in, tasting her. She felt as if she might just seep into his very soul. "How about this?" He asked when he finally tore his mouth from hers. His voice rang husky and thick in her ears. "*Ti amo con tutto il cuore e con tutta l'anima.*"

Robin looked into his eyes and saw the seriousness of whatever he was saying. She tried to pick through the words, find something that sounded familiar so that she could translate it. Did he just...? "Say it again," she demanded.

"*Ti amo con tutto il cuore e con tutta l'anima.*" She started quaking inside of her stomach. His hands moved from her face down her neck until they rested on her shoulders. "I love you, Robin... with all of my heart and soul."

The quaking left her stomach and radiated out to her limbs. With shaking hands she cupped his cheeks. "Tony," she said, trying to talk around the huge smile on her face, around the nervous laughter bubbling up in her throat. "I realized I was in love with you the day of your party, but then Craig came and..." she stopped, not wanting to babble incessantly. "Let me try," she said.

He cupped her hands with his and pulled them off of his face. Keeping one hand gripped in his, he stepped back a bit while her inexperienced tongue fumbled on the words. "*Ti amo, con tat,* no." she said, then gasped as he slipped the ring on her finger.

"*Con tutto il cuore e con tutta l'anima.*" He finished for her. Trapping her eyes with his, he slowly descended until one knee rested on the sandy beach. "Marry me, Robin. Make my life complete."

"I—I—" She couldn't tear her eyes off the sapphire.

Tony's face, always so stoic and guarded, could be read by anyone who saw it. He looked at her with naked need and tender hope. "I love you, *cara.* I don't think that there was a moment in my life that made me happier than the day that you came to know Christ, the day that you gave your life over to the Lord. If you would do me the honor of being my wife..." He stopped and closed his eyes.

Holding her hand, he ran his thumb over the ring. "Let me love you in every way God commanded a man to love his wife. Let me treasure you, and abide in you, and protect you, and honor you."

The quaking subsided. Peace flooded over her body, warmed her from the inside out. "Yes," she said through the tears that fell unencumbered down her cheeks. He stood and their eyes came back to even again. She laughed and grabbed him and hugged him. "Yes, of course. Of course I'll be your wife."

He wrapped both of his arms around her and hugged her tightly to him, lifting her up from the sand and spinning them both around until he felt the wet surf beneath his feet. As he gently returned her to earth, his lips found hers and they kissed, standing in the sand with the water swirling at their ankles.

THE END OF *Sapphire Ice*

CHAPTER ONE

R obin **Bartlett walked into** her church's main fellowship hall and surveyed the crowd. People young and old, fellow congregates, had gathered on that second Sunday afternoon in January to celebrate the engagement of Robin and Antonio "Tony" Viscolli. Everyone brought a covered dish to create a pot luck meal of such amazing amplitude that Robin wondered if the table would bow under the weight.

She could hear the clanging of dishes in the kitchen and started to step in that direction, but Tony slipped his hand into hers and halted her forward progress. She turned and looked at her handsome fiancé in his navy suit, white shirt, and red tie, looking every bit the Italian businessman. He stood barely an inch taller than her almost six feet. She knew she complemented him with her blonde hair and fair skin. This morning she wore a blue sweater dress the color of her eyes, belted at the waist with a silver belt that matched her shoes. No one meeting either one of them would know that they grew up on the streets in the same harsh Boston neighborhood around where this very church stood. "This is your party, *cara*. Let them bless you. Stay out here and socialize."

Leaning toward him so that only he could hear her, she whispered, "I'm not very good at that."

He smiled, a smile that made her heart pitter-patter in her chest and made her fall in love with him all over again. He raised her hand and kissed it just above the ridiculously large oval sapphire and diamond ring on her left hand. "You'll get better at it. You are positively beautiful and engaging. Everyone is looking forward to visiting with you."

She had started attending the church just a few months before, but Tony had attended for years. He had entered the church as a desperate, starving teen years before, looking for something to steal and fence. Instead he had heard the Gospel message and ended up dedicating his life to the Creator of the universe.

Tony knew so many people in that room, and Robin knew a select handful. Still, he looked so excited to introduce her around and let her meet the people who mattered the most in his life, she let go of her feelings of insecurity and walked from group to group, table to table, meeting friends and the family members of friends, watching her future husband talk to even the people he didn't know well with grace and with caring compassion. It was so easy to stand at his side and engage in conversation with everyone. Tony made it easy.

They worked their way through the room to the table of food and filled their plates. Tony, with his gold cufflinks and diamond pinkie ring looked out of place carrying a foam paper plate with a white plastic fork. Robin smiled as she sat in the metal folding chair next to him.

"There is so much food here," she observed, looking at her plate and thinking she might have overdone it on the *little bit here and little bit there* strategy. "Everything looks so amazing."

"I love potluck dinners," he said. "It's almost like a treasure hunt."

Robin laughed and laid her hand on top of his, gently squeezing. "That's a good way to look at it."

She dug into her food. She'd felt so nervous about today's party that she'd been unable to eat breakfast that morning. As she finished the impossibly full plate, she eyed the crowded dessert table and wondered if she dared.

Tony saw her glance and winked. "I'll go get you something. Chocolate?"

Robin leaned back in her chair and sighed. "I shouldn't but, yes. Definitely."

As he walked away, someone gripped her shoulders from behind. Robin turned and found herself in the presence of both of her younger half-sisters, Maxine and Sarah. Maxine had glided up behind her.

"I'm so sorry we're late," Maxine said, setting her purse on the seat next to Robin's. "Sarah's church service ran way over."

At twenty-six, blonde-haired, blue-eyed Robin was the oldest of the three half-sisters. Her father had spent her childhood in prison for trafficking cocaine.

Green-eyed Maxine was three years younger than Robin. Her nameless father had been a warm bed on a drunken night for their addicted mother. Only Maxine's Native American features and straight black hair gave evidence to which of the many one-night-stands had fathered her. Maxine was currently a junior associate at a Boston advertising agency.

Petite Sarah had honey-colored eyes and wild curly auburn hair. Her father had committed suicide when she was just a baby. Robin remembered him as one of the only nice men who had ever come into her childhood life. Now twenty-years-old, Sarah was in her third year of college and her first year of nursing school.

After a horrible night when their mother and the latest boyfriend had fallen victim to murder, a family had adopted Sarah while Robin and Maxine landed in the foster system. The older sisters had no contact with Sarah until her fifteenth birthday. She now lived with Robin and Maxine while her older sister paid for her college education.

Robin eyed her watch. "That's okay," she said, "I'm so happy you could make it."

"I tried to tell her to skip her parents' church this morning and just come here, but she had a thing."

Sarah rolled her eyes and pushed her glasses further up her tiny nose. "I teach a Sunday school class, Maxi. I can't very well just skip that."

Robin interjected, trying to stop the bickering before it unfolded into a full-blown argument. "It's cool. You didn't miss anything important. I'm just so happy you're here." She waved a hand in the general direction of the heavy-laden table. "Help yourself to food."

Maxine pushed away from the table and went behind Robin's chair, slipping her arms around her older sister's neck and hugging her. "I'm so excited for you. I just love Tony."

Robin grinned. "Yeah? Me, too."

As soon as Maxine let her go, Sarah hugged her. "Me, three. And, I'm thankful that you're back in my life. I was thinking about it this morning, about all those years I didn't even know you existed. I wish I'd grown up with you like Maxi did. You are amazing and I just love you so much."

Robin had never heard anything like that from Sarah before. Emotion, raw and real, swamped her and her eyes burned with tears. She pushed away from the table and pulled Sarah into her arms. "I'm glad you don't remember," she said, resting her cheek on top of her youngest sister's head. "I'm glad you're saved from that, and I'm so happy you live with me now. It helps make up for lost time."

As Sarah followed Maxine to the buffet tables, Tony returned with a too-large slice of chocolate cake. "Your cake, my love," he announced with flare.

He looked at her face and a frown immediately appeared between his brows. "Why are you crying?"

Robin took his face in her hands. "Because God has blessed me with such love in abundance. I don't even know how to begin to thank Him."

Tony put a hand on top of hers. "We'll work together for Him and serve Him. That's how."

Not caring how many hundreds of eyes might be watching, Robin leaned forward and kissed him, just a quick brush of her lips on his. "I'm looking forward to it."

Maxine returned with a plate piled high with food, followed by Sarah who had a bit of salad and some steamed broccoli on her plate. As Sarah sat down, she said, "Not many options for the herbivores among us," she said with a smile. "Pot luck suppers at churches are always full of meat and cheese."

Maxine took a bite of a chicken leg. "Ah. That's the good stuff," she said with a smile. She pointed the leg at Robin and Tony, who sat back down across from them. "Have you two set a date in stone yet?"

Robin grinned the silly grin that kept spreading across her face ever since Tony put the ring on her finger. "April twenty-first is about the soonest it can possibly be."

Tony rubbed the back of her neck. "Robin suggested we just elope, but I convinced her that I was worth a church wedding."

With a fork laden with potato salad, Maxine said, "You don't want to elope. There's no fun in that. I know I'll never elope."

"Oh, I don't know." Wiggling his eyebrows, Tony said, "It could be fun."

Sarah swallowed a laugh and covered her mouth. "Tony!"

Barry Anderson, former professional football player turned corporate lawyer, walked up to Tony, wool ski cap covering his ears and leather gloves on his large hands. He slapped Tony on the back. "My friend, congratulations."

Tony smiled and stood, shamelessly hugging Barry. "Barry, *mio fratello*!" He turned and faced the table. "Barry, my dearest brother, I would like to introduce you to Maxine Bartlett and Sarah Thomas, Robin's sisters." The two best friends could not have more different appearances. Barry stood a few inches shy of seven feet with icy blue eyes, blond hair, a thin blond goatee, and a body that gave evidence to his extensive workout regimen compared to Tony who stood at just six feet with dark coloring and a strong lean body strengthened by rowing. And yet they considered themselves brothers as if they'd been born to the same parents.

Sarah was closest, and reached forward to shake Barry's hand. He slipped the glove off of his right hand and gripped her petite hand, swamping it. Maxine, her eyes uncharacteristically wide, made no move to rise or shake his hand. She just said, "Nice to meet you."

"I should have realized Robin's sisters would be just as lovely and beautiful as Robin. It is very much my honor to finally meet you both." Barry nodded to each of them and looked them straight in the eye as he greeted them. Then he turned back to Tony. "Sorry I'm late. The flight out was delayed almost two hours."

"That big storm?" Tony inquired.

"Yeah. The snow has really been picking up. We passed 12 or 15 foot drifts on the way to the airport. I guess it's a good thing we made it out at all."

Tony nodded. "How was Christmas in the Alps?"

Barry's lips thinned. "Same thing every year."

"You should really think about Florida next year." Tony chided. "You could water ski off the Keys instead of making snow angels."

Barry kept his face blank. "Maybe next year." He pulled his ski cap off and gestured to the buffet table. "I'm going to get something to eat. That little plate they give you on the airline is never enough for me."

As he walked away, Maxine leaned in to Robin and said in a low voice, "Do you know who that is? That is *the* Barry Anderson."

"Yeah, that's Barry. I told you about him helping my dad."

Maxine lightly thumped her sister on the forehead with her flat open palm. "No. That is Barry 'The Bear' Anderson. Like, that is really, really him. Don't you remember him playing? Remember the Super Bowl that year? Are you really that out of it?"

"Yes. And I remember telling you that he used to play sports and he's a lawyer, now." Robin said, feeling a little confused.

Maxine grinned. "Play sports. You are so cute. You said he was a big guy and a lawyer and drank Shirley Temples. I was imagining fat Elvis meets Perry Mason meets Freddie Mercury. You never said anything about him being *that* Barry Anderson. You know I had the biggest crush on him when he was in the League. And he is still the most gorgeous man I've ever seen in my life." She put her hand on her chest. "Oh my gosh. I can barely breathe."

Robin's eyes widened and she laughed a shocked laugh. "You are incorrigible."

Maxine winked and went back to her plate.

Tony's lips thinned as he stood again. "Good afternoon, Jacqui."

A tall redhead with porcelain smooth skin sailed toward their table, draped in a full length mink coat. "Antonio, what a pleasure to see you," she said, air kissing within inches of both of his cheeks.

"Ladies, I'd like you to meet Barry's wife, Jacqueline Anderson. Jacqui, this is Sarah Thomas, Maxine Bartlett, and my beautiful bride to be, Robin Bartlett."

She waved a hand toward Robin. "You are *such* a darling. Bartlett. Bartlett? Now, are your people any relation to the Chesapeake Bartletts?"

Maxine dryly interjected, "I seriously doubt it."

Jacqueline took that in. "Hmm. Well, it is just so very nice to meet you in person." Robin stood next to Tony and held her hand out. Jacqueline slipped off her gloves. Robin thought her long manicured nails made her hands look like she'd never worked a day in her life. The women briefly squeezed hands and Tony gestured to the buffet line. "Barry's fixing himself a plate. Would you care to eat?"

A quick look of disgust crossed her face as she surveyed either her husband or the selections on his plate.

"Ugh. Church food. Not the slightest bit interested." She put a hand on Tony's shoulder. "I'm afraid I can't stay, Antonio. I just had to pop in and say 'hi.' My curiosity was positively killing me as to who finally landed the most eligible bachelor I know and snagged you right out from under the noses of Boston society!"

At the conclusion of this announcement, Jacqueline Anderson actually looked Robin up and down from head to toe as if inspecting a Dickensian orphan or a horse of questionable pedigree. "I'm so looking forward to the wedding. The papers are already talking about how it's going to be the event of the year." She nodded toward Barry, who had stopped on his way back to the table to talk to Peter O'Farrell. "Be a dear and tell Barry I'll see him later. I simply must go, now."

She swirled away, leaving the cloying smell of expensive French perfume in her wake. Robin slowly sat as she watched her mink clad departure for a second, then her eyes skimmed over Barry, who'd barely glanced at his wife's retreating back before continuing his conversation with Peter. She looked at Tony. "What was that?"

Tony lifted his red plastic cup. "That, *cara*, was Jacqui Anderson, in all her glory, being just as nice as she is humanly able."

With an astonished tone, she asked, "And—Antonio?"

Tony actually grit his teeth. "It doesn't bother me, but that fact doesn't seem to stop her from trying to make it bother me."

Maxine set her fork down. "Wow."

Tony patted the back of Robin's hand. "She will be extremely helpful in the wedding planning. She is a master at events. Just... don't let her bully you."

Maxine wasn't done. "You know what? I'll say that

backwards. Wow. There."

Robin took a bite of her cake, letting the chocolate frosting sing in her mouth before slowly chewing it and swallowing. She washed down that bite with a sip from a cup of really bad coffee in a white Styrofoam cup. "What did she mean by 'the event of the year?' She made this sound like it was going to be the next Royal Wedding."

Tony waved his hand in a dismissive manner as Barry set his plate next to him. "Don't let that bother you, *cara*."

"I think the event of the year is exactly what it should be," Sarah said dreamily. "Imagine what we could do!"

Maxine leaned forward and put her hand on top of Robin's. "It's okay, Robin. We'll help you. We'll get a really good wedding planner and it'll be a breeze. I even have an old design instructor from college who opened her business last year. I helped her with some initial advertising. I'll call her and see if we can meet."

Suddenly nervous, Robin licked her lips. "I'm not sure. Why can't we just elope?"

Tony laughed. "Because, *cara*, I want to show you off to the world." He turned to Barry. "You free in the morning? I have some things to go over with you."

Barry nodded around a mouth full of cauliflower casserole. "I have you blocked off until noon. After that, you're buying me lunch. I've been out of the office for two weeks. I'll go in at seven and make sure I don't have any major fires to put out before I come over."

Tony nodded as he looked at his watch. "Nine is good." He snapped his fingers and turned to Robin. "I know what I forgot to tell you."

"What?"

"You need to go ahead and get your passport application turned in. It takes several weeks, and I don't want to delay our honeymoon."

Her mouth felt a little dry as she contemplated, suddenly, all of the details she'd need to handle in the next four months. She barely heard him. "Passport?"

"Yes. To go to Italy. Remember?"

Mind whirling, wishing she had a pencil and a paper to take notes, she nodded. "Right, Italy."

He frowned. "You okay?"

She shook her head and nodded. "Just a little overwhelmed. I need to remember where my birth certificate is, too."

Tony took her hand and kissed the back of it. "Relax, my love. All will be fine. I promise."

CHAPTER TWO

Tony paused in working his way through the stack of end-of-the-year and fourth quarter revenue reports when his secretary, Margaret, buzzed through on the intercom. "Mr. Viscolli, there's a young man coming up who has a business card with a handwritten note from you on the back of it."

A happy relief flooded his chest. "Yes, Derrick. I remember him. Please have the chef send up some hearty hot food and some hot tea. Maybe hot chocolate, too. He's going to be cold and hungry."

He felt relieved to have a break. For the first time in nearly three years, Tony faced the unappealing prospect of having to instigate some layoffs. One of his West Coast endeavors was still infuriatingly and stubbornly unprofitable. The problem was that the project was currently overstaffed. But Tony had a stubborn streak of his own. From a public image perspective, he couldn't lay his reputation on the line and layoff nearly 200 workers right before Christmas then turn around and employ at least that number of staff to pull off his wedding and reception a few months down the road. From another perspective, he realized that his employees had families and financial obligations and depended on his company to meet their needs.

But for the last two years, he had been throwing money at that company with no tangible profitable return. Half a year ago, the tax write off and depreciation options had stopped being very much fun. The bottom line was that it would have to turn around before the end of first quarter next year, or else he would have to write it off as a complete loss. Since that wasn't an option, he had to get creative. He was going to have to pray long and hard about the problem.

Tony had time to file the reports away and make sure nothing pressing waited for him on his desk. Closing his eyes, he uttered a brief prayer, "Please God, help me focus on this meeting and let me make a difference in this young man's life."

As he raised his head, a knock sounded on his door. Margaret opened it without waiting for him to bid entrance, and in walked Derrick DiNunzio.

He had lost weight in the weeks since Tony first met him outside of a dirty bar in the absolutely wrong neighborhood. Tony had looked at the teenage boy with bloody knuckles and dirt on his face and seen a reflection of himself not long before. Then something, the Holy Spirit he supposed, pressed him to help this young man. He told Derrick to come see him when he turned eighteen. Now Derrick stood before him, right there in the same black leather jacket with the hole in the elbow, dirty jeans, worn out boots, and red-rimmed eyes. He had a scruffy beard and chapped lips.

"Derrick DiNunzio," Tony said, stepping forward with his hand out. Derrick looked at it and hesitantly shook it. Tony gripped Derrick's hand with his other hand, trying to convey friendship and warmth. "I'm pleased you decided to take me up on my offer and come see me."

Derrick shrugged and tried to act tough, but he kept looking around at the very large and well appointed office. "Yeah, well you said maybe you had a job for me, Mr. Viscolli, and I could really use the work, so I came."

Tony looked at Margaret over Derrick's shoulder. "Just go ahead and bring in the food when it arrives if you could, Margaret."

"Yes, sir," she said, closing the door behind her.

Tony gestured to the brown leather couch and chairs that formed a sitting area near a lit fireplace. "Please, sit down, Derrick."

Derrick shoved his hands in his pockets and slouched toward the couch. "What kind of job you need me to do, Mr. Viscolli?"

Tony ignored the question and sat in a chair facing Derrick. "*Lei parla italiano?*"

The youth shook his head. "Nah. My mom, she didn't speak English and she wanted to learn. By the time I was old enough to talk, she refused to teach me any except when she was cussing me out."

"Well, cussing does sound more sincere in Italian, doesn't it?"

"I never questioned her sincerity, Mr. Viscolli."

Tony chuckled. "That's too bad. I was hoping to knock some of the rust off my Italian while we talked. I guess it will have to wait until my honeymoon." He sat back and hooked his foot on his knee, brushing an imaginary piece of lint off of the gray silk pants leg.

"Yeah, I saw in the Globe about you getting married. No disrespect. She looks smokin' hot. Like, smokin'. Congrats."

Once more it struck Tony just how much this young man reflected a younger version of himself. He vividly remembered—not so very long ago—having a very similar outlook and nearly identical priorities. What he couldn't have realized is how much better his life could be when he stopped trying to run it himself and instead gave his life up to Christ.

With a little smile, Tony said, "None taken. And I agree. She is the most beautiful woman I've ever seen. So, you have a mother. Who else is in your family?"

"Just me." Derrick's eyes narrowed. "Why ya asking?"

"I am a curious man. My mother was alone when she came to Boston, pregnant with me. Her family had disowned her in Florence and my father had a great aunt here so she came to America. To say she was disappointed in our neighborhood is not an exaggeration."

Derrick cocked his head. "My mom was from Naples."

"Ah. *Napoli*." Tony did a quick calculation. "Navy brat?"

"Air Force." Derrick crossed his arms and leaned back. "Knocked her up, brought her here, then dumped her. She didn't know anything about getting the military to track him down or nothing. Found out too late. He's dead, now. I never met him."

"In our neighborhood, that is nothing new."

"You say 'our' like you're still there. But, you're not. You got out."

Tony shrugged. "Not entirely. I still go to church near there, and I do a lot of community work there. But, you're right, I no longer live there."

"Again, no disrespect, Mr. Viscolli, but you don't even sound like you ever lived in Southie."

With a wave of his hand, Tony dismissed that remark. "That just takes hard work. I hired someone to teach me how to speak properly."

Derrick gestured with his chin. "And the suits."

"Right. That, too." He tapped a finger on the arm of his chair. "I have to maintain a certain look in order to do good business. That may or may not be 'right' on some fundamental level, but it is the way the world works. I recognized that and conformed." He thought back to his teenage years. It might as well have been him sitting in that chair instead of young Derrick DiNunzio. God had given him a chance, and he would do the same for this young man. "My last winter on the streets, I slept in the doorway of that old brick building near that pasta place, Buenos. You know where I'm talking about?"

Derrick uncrossed his arms. "Slept? Yeah, I know the spot. There's an old dude who sleeps there, named—"

"Georgio," Tony interrupted. "Yes. He gave me tips for surviving the winter. Glad to hear he's still alive. One of his tips was to go into churches during services to get warm. A lot of churches serve coffee and pastries afterward, too. I went into Boston Central Bible Church one cold night and it changed my life forever."

Margaret entered, pushing a service cart. Tony stood and thanked her, taking the cart from her and rolling it to where Derrick sat. He lifted the silver dome off a plate and found roast beef with mashed potatoes and green peas. Bless Margaret, he thought, who knew, despite the early hour, to bring something other than croissants and fruit. He set the plate in front of Derrick. He watched the boy's hungry face light up and heard the audible sound of his stomach growling. He quickly poured him a cup of hot tea and sat down. "Let me bless this food before you eat," he said, not handing over the silverware wrapped in a cloth napkin just yet. He bowed his head and said, very quickly so that he did not torture the boy, "Father God, thank You for working in our lives and bringing Derrick and me together. I pray You bless this food to the nourishment of our bodies. In Your holy name we pray, Amen."

He handed Derrick the bundle of utensils and sat back with his own cup of tea while the young man attacked the plate of food. When it was empty, he lifted the dome on another identical plate and set that in front of him as well. This time, he ate more slowly.

"What do you mean, it changed your life?" Derrick asked with his mouth full.

"What?"

"The church. How did church do anything for you? Never did nothin' for me I tell ya that."

"Ah." Tony smiled and poured more tea for both of them. "Let me tell you a story about forgiveness and redemption."

ROBIN'S worn out car shuddered to a stop about 12 feet shy of the valet stand in front of the Boston Viscolli Hotel. She opened the door before the valet could get to her. "I'm so sorry, Ryan," she said, her cheeks burning with embarrassment. "I hope you can get it started."

"No problem, Miss Bartlett," he said smoothly. "We'll take care of it for you. Please don't concern yourself."

Rushing, she opened the back door and grabbed her purse and notepad, then slammed it shut and hit it with her hip to make sure it latched. She knew she was going to have to replace this car, and soon. The cold winter seemed to bring out the worst in the machine. Since her promotion from head bartender to restaurant manager at Hank's Place, she finally had the extra money to put away and had been saving for a more reliable used car, but she didn't have enough put aside yet. She had to limp the thing along for just another couple of months.

The frigid Boston wind bit at her cheeks and she rushed into the warm lobby of the hotel. Most people working there knew her by now. Tony's executive offices were on the top floor of the hotel, and she had been there several times in the last few months. She thought back to the first time she'd come there, how angry she'd been at Tony, how offended by him. Now she came in smiling, walking on air, coming to meet Maxine and a wedding planner, saying, "Hi," to the people she knew personally and basking in their smiles and returned greetings.

Green marble, shiny brass, brown leather, thick oriental rugs—it all worked together to create an atmosphere of luxury and style. As many times as she'd come through those doors, she still didn't stop from marveling at the ambiance. It was so beautiful and so rich feeling. Furniture was arranged in different seating areas around the lobby, and Robin wove her way through to the fireplace, where she'd arranged to meet the wedding planner.

A tall woman in a red suit with silver hair in a tight bun stood next to the hearth. Robin went straight for her. "Stephanie?" she said, holding out her hand, "I'm Robin. I'm so sorry I'm late."

If Maxine were already there, Robin imagined her sister would offer something very droll along the lines of, "Car trouble?"

Stephanie looked her up and down, from the toes of her brown boots, past her jeans and Harvard sweatshirt, to the top of her head, where she had her long blonde hair pulled back in a pony tail. "Robin Bartlett?" Stephanie asked. "I never would have guessed you were Maxine's sister."

Used to such confusion about their looks, Robin said, "I look like our mom. She looks like her dad." She waved at her outfit. "Sorry I'm so dressed down. I've been in the freezer of my restaurant since four this morning trying to organize a meat delivery." She pushed her coat off of her shoulders as a uniformed concierge approached. She held it out to him with a smile and continued speaking. "We were up to our eyeballs in Angus steaks and I didn't hear the alarm on my phone going off reminding me of this breakfast."

Stephanie smiled, but Robin could read the hesitation on her face. Then she asked, "Are they going to let you in? Isn't there a dress code in the restaurant?"

"It's not a problem." She gestured toward the restaurant. "Maxine will be here shortly. She got tied up in traffic. Cassandra texted me that she had a table waiting for us in the restaurant. Maxine will just meet us there."

"I've worked with Cassandra here before," Stephanie said as they approached the hostess stand. "She is one of the most helpful entertainment coordinators in any hotel around Boston."

"I know. Tony can't say enough about her."

Stephanie put a hand on Robin's arm. "Wait, Tony?"

Robin raised an eyebrow as the hostess approached. "Yeah, Tony. Tony Viscolli. My fiancé."

"*You* are Tony Viscolli's fiancée? How did I miss that?"

With a shrug, Robin laughed. "You never asked." She

turned to the hostess. "Hi, Amy."

"Hi, Robin. Cassandra is already waiting for you. Right this way, please."

Cassandra smiled and held out her hand as Robin approached. "Hi, Robin. It's nice to meet you in person."

"Likewise," she said as she shook the brunette's hand. Cassandra had a round face with dimples that lit her face up when she smiled. Robin gestured at Stephanie. "You've met Stephanie Giordano. She's still reeling over the fact that she's going to be working on the Viscolli wedding."

"The Bartlett-Viscolli wedding," Cassandra enthused.

Stephanie sat across from Cassandra. "I guess I'd read your name in the paper, but never associated it with Maxine. When she called, she wasn't specific." She asked for a diet soda from the waitress and continued. "I am so honored to be asked to do this."

Maxine breezed toward their table, well over six-feet-tall in her three-inch boots, suede skirt, and silk blouse. "Sorry! There was a tow truck—oh, never mind." She said as she took the chair across from Robin. "It's good to see you all." She looked at the waitress who had finished taking drink orders. "Coffee please, black."

Stephanie pulled out her tablet and set it on the table in front of her, wiping some lint from the screen before waking it up. "April 21st?"

Robin nodded. "Yes. We're thinking late afternoon with a reception early evening."

"How many guests?" Stephanie asked while nodding and typing.

Robin deferred to Cassandra. "How many can we accommodate here?"

"We're going to use the Grand Ball Room. I can fit up to seven-fifty and maintain fire-code. We can also open the doors and use the patio area. And, we can bring in heated tents if we need to."

Stephanie paused, fingers on the screen. "Seven hundred and fifty?" She repeated in a near whisper.

Maxine laughed. "Think of the Viscolli wedding on your company's resume."

"Bartlett-Viscolli wedding," Cassandra corrected automatically.

Robin felt her heart skitter. Her mouth went dry and she suddenly felt overwhelmed by the concept. Trying to clear her head, she gave it a short shake. "Seven hundred and fifty people? Seriously?"

Maxine reached over and took her hand. "Easily. Just think of the church congregates alone. Tony's managers and supervisors, their spouses or guests, all of his ministries, his business contacts. I bet we reach a thousand before it's all done."

Cassandra opened her notebook. "We need to set a number now, if it's possible. I need to make sure I can accommodate with table settings and staff."

Robin held up a hand. "Let's limit it to what will fit inside. That will keep it simple."

"Okay, seven-fifty. Easily done." Cassandra wrote on a legal pad with a fine-tip pen while Stephanie typed.

"We need a guest list soon," Stephanie said. "That's a lot of envelopes to address. I will likely hire that out."

"Tony's secretary is already working on it," Cassandra said. "Her name is Margaret. I'll get you her contact info."

Stephanie jumped. "Oh, right. Here's my card."

Cassandra nodded. "And here's mine."

The women handed out business cards all around then Stephanie turned back to Robin. "Give me some ideas of what you're thinking about in terms of style or theme."

Robin raised an eyebrow. "Style?"

Maxine interjected, "She wants simple but elegant. Nothing ostentatious but nothing flashy, either. No swans or doves. Like they say in showbiz, never follow children or animals. And no elaborate foods, just tasteful simple fare."

Stephanie nodded and typed. Cassandra asked, "Are you going to do sit-down dinner?"

Finally, something to which she could speak with authority due to her years as a waitress. "Yes. But, I don't want to have too many choices for people. I want to do a small red meat, like maybe lamb, and a small poultry portion on the same plate with two simple sides. That will save the chefs a lot of headache and ensure that meals are set out hot. I do want to accommodate vegetarians if we need to, and make sure the vegetarian plates are fully organic, only fruits and vegetables with whole grains. Nothing processed at all, especially soy. Oh, maybe a nice tomato soup or consommé. My sister, Sarah, will thank us."

While Cassandra made notes, the waitress arrived with drinks and took their breakfast orders. As they waited for meals to arrive, Robin and Maxine—mainly Maxine—answered questions and let Stephanie and Cassandra work between them to get the initial outline of their planning started. Robin pondered just how quickly four short months could pass. How would they ever get it all done on time?

ROBIN hugged Maxine good-bye and watched her get into her little green sports car. After three hours of meeting with such competent women who seemed to know exactly what to say and do, she felt a little less overwhelmed by the process, but still a little anxious about the timing. Maybe Tony would consider pushing the wedding back to June. Or maybe next January. That would be even better. Or maybe they could just go to a Justice of the Peace and that would be that. Better still.

Shaking her head, knowing he wanted to get married as soon as possible and in their church, she waited for the valet, who pulled up in a sleek and shiny royal blue sedan. He walked toward her. "Hi, Ryan. Did you get it started?"

"Mr. V. took care of it, Robin."

She waited, but he didn't move. After several heartbeats, she said, "I don't understand."

He pointed with his thumb over his shoulder. "That's yours, now, ma'am."

His thumb loosely pointed at a brand new four door sedan that looked like it had just rolled off of a high end showroom. Robin shook her head. "No, it's not."

"Yes, ma'am. Your other car was towed away and this one was brought in. The stuff that was in your trunk and back seat has already been transferred." He held out brand new shiny car keys that were absolutely not hers hanging on her key chain beside her apartment key and the keys to Hank's place.

She suddenly remembered Maxine mentioning a tow truck. Nice of her sister not to mention that her car was strapped to it. Without another word, Robin pivoted on her heel with military precision and marched back into the hotel. She stalked to the elevators and hit the top floor button harder than she should have. Thankfully, she had no wait and the elevator shot up twenty stories with efficient speed, but the ride seemed interminable to her.

The receptionist sitting behind a large half-moon desk saw her and smiled. "Good afternoon, Miss Bartlett," she greeted.

Robin nodded but did not speak. Instead, she stormed off the elevator and into the lobby of the office floor. She barely realized that her feet sank into the lush carpet nor did she pay any attention to the leather furniture and black granite tables.

Her eyes caught the scrolling brass on the wall behind the desk that read: *He has showed you, O man, what is good. And what does the Lord require of you? To act justly and to love mercy and to walk humbly with your God. Micah 6:8.*

She proceeded down the corridor and entered Tony's outer office. His secretary sat poised with hands on her keyboard but looked up when Robin entered. "Hello, Robin," Margaret said with a smile. "Mr. Viscolli will certainly be happy to see you."

"I doubt it," she said through gritted teeth. "Is he available?"

"He is in this morning, but he has someone in there. Let me call him out." She stood and walked around her desk, stopping at the large double oak doors. With a quick tap, she opened the door a crack and stuck her head in, speaking in a low tone. As she finished speaking, she stepped back and the doors opened wider.

Tony came out, looking like he had just stepped out of a shoot for the cover of a fashion magazine in his gray silk suit and dark green tie. He grinned and held his hands out to her. "*Cara*, my love. What a wonderful surprise."

Robin held her hands up to ward him off. "Where did you take my car?"

Tony stopped and raised his eyebrows, slipping his hands into his pockets. "Ah, so it's like that is it?" His smile grew infuriatingly broad. "I seem to remember the first time you ever came to this office. You threw a fist full of money at my chest like throwing a stone. Are we to metaphorically commemorate that act? Is today an anniversary or something?"

"Tony, where is my car?"

He gestured toward some double doors on the other side of the room. "Let's take this conversation into my conference room."

Robin stormed behind him and waited to speak until he had shut the door. "Answer me. Right now. Where is my car?"

"You mean where is that rusty junk heap that refused to start and had to be towed away?"

"Yeah, I mean *my* rusty junk heap that you had towed without my permission."

"I stand corrected. *Your* rusty, unreliable, and unsafe junk heap is at a mechanic's shop. I had a feeling you wouldn't approve of the new car, so I'm getting the old one fixed until I can charm you into accepting the gift of your new car." He smiled an endearing smile that started to melt her anger.

"Charm me?" She shook her head. "I don't want cars from you, Tony."

"I know that, Robin. I also don't care," He held up a hand, palm facing her, at her gasp. "Understand that my wife, when she becomes my wife, will drive a safe and reliable car that will not break down on her. Ever. Because, you see, I will take my God ordained responsibilities to my wife very seriously. My wife will be protected and provided for in a way that glorifies our Creator's design for husbands and wives. And as for giving you gifts, I cannot imagine a time when that will ever stop. You are the love of my life and I would give you the moon and stars."

Robin took a deep breath and released it. She rubbed her forehead. "Can we just wait to do things like buy me expensive new cars and such until after we're married? We aren't married yet, and I really, really don't feel right about this."

Tony stepped forward and put his hands on her shoulders. "We are married in my heart. The rest is just ceremony and tradition. But, yes, of course. We can wait. Your car should be back soon. Apparently, it only needs the engine and transmission replaced. And new tires, of course." She stepped forward and let him wrap her up in his arms. He smelled so good, and she buried her face in his neck and just breathed. "And brakes. And that back door and window fixed. Just a few details like that."

"Tony…" she warned.

Tony cleared his throat. "*Cara*, I need to talk to you about something. A bit more serious than your inexplicable anger that I took care of your car for you, if I may."

She lifted her head, but before she could step back, he framed her face with his hands and leaned forward and kissed her. She wondered if there would ever come a day that the feel of his lips didn't warm her body all the way to her soul. Would her heart ever not pause between beats in her chest just long enough to trip forward at an impossible rate? Would her skin ever not tingle for want of his touch? As she stepped closer and deepened the kiss, her arms slipped around his neck and she sighed.

Tony lifted his head and looked at her, his eyes so dark they looked nearly black. He stared at her for a long time before giving her another quick kiss and stepping away.

Robin smiled. "You need to talk to me about something?"

"Yes." He pulled out a chair at the conference table and gestured toward it. Robin sat down and he sat next to her. "Last month, when I was in my old neighborhood, I met a boy. A young man, that is."

Robin grimaced, knowing exactly why he'd been in that neighborhood. "Go on."

"The Holy Spirit spoke to me, almost audibly, and told me to reach out to him. I gave him my card and told him to come see me when he turned eighteen. His birthday was yesterday."

Robin cocked her head, a little confused. "Did he come see you?"

"Yes. He's been here since about eight-thirty."

"And?"

Tony reached for her hand. She placed it in his. He ran his thumb over the sapphire. "And, I'm going to bring him home with me tonight. I've been gutting the apartment rooms, prepping for you and your sisters. Maxine let me know at church Sunday that she will not be moving in with us because she's purchasing that place on Newbury Street. Since I'd already started the work on a suite of rooms for her, I have the space nearly ready. I'm going to offer him a job and a home."

She felt her eyes widen. "Wow." Knowing people, and the neighborhood where Tony met this boy, she leaned forward. "Is this wise?"

Tony smiled and ran a finger down her cheek. "Is it wise to listen to the counsel of the Holy Spirit? I feel good saying yes to that."

Robin sandwiched his hand with both of hers. "Then I trust you, and Him." She smiled. "You are a good man, and I love your heart. I can't wait to marry you."

Tony brought her hands up to his mouth and kissed

each one. "Thank you, *cara*. You do my heart good."

She stood. "I'll let you get back to him. What is his name?"

"Derrick." He stood with her. "Derrick DiNunzio. If you can meet us at the apartment in a couple of hours, that would be wonderful. My interior designer is there with a few contractors working as quickly as possible to get a room ready for him. I'm sure she'd appreciate some authoritative direction."

She mentally rearranged her day. "Okay. I'll go by there."

"Can you enlist Maxine? He'll need clothes. She might enjoy taking him shopping with my credit card."

"I'll call her as soon as I get to the car." She put a hand on his cheek and leaned forward, pressing her lips to his. "Don't forget that I want my old car back."

Tony sighed. "I haven't forgotten. I'll wait to have it crushed until the day after we get married."

She laughed as she put her purse over her shoulder. "Don't say that too loud before the wedding or she might not start anymore." She headed toward the door and paused. "Oh, before I forget, you're limited to 750 wedding guests."

"Oh? Just 750 couples? That should be fine."

"No, Tony, 750 total guests."

With a raised eyebrow, he said, "*Non possibile.*"

"Well, you're just going to have to make it possible, mister."

Tony's laugh barked around the room. "Very well. I shall limit it. Let Margaret know. She'll have to start cutting down the invite list."

CHAPTER THREE

Robin and Maxine stepped off the elevator and into Tony's apartment. It took up the entire top floor of the building—space equal to four luxurious penthouse apartments. They stepped down from the entrance into a huge great room with a glass wall that looked out over the city. A large circular sectional couch and a low square coffee table created a sitting area. Double doors on one end of the room led through the dining room into the kitchen, and a wide hall on the other end led to four bedroom and bathroom suites.

Maxine looked right, then left, then up. "I should reconsider and move in here. Is it too late? It's too late, isn't it?"

Robin walked in the middle of the room and turned in a circle. This was only her second visit to Tony's apartment. A middle aged woman wearing designer jeans and a plaid flannel shirt with white hair falling out of a sloppy bun on the top of her head came out of the hallway and rushed into the room.

"Robin? Hello, I'm Betty." She went straight for Robin, with her hand extended. Then she looked at Maxine. "You must be the sister. Maxine, right? So pleased to meet you both." When her hand was free, she gestured toward the hallway. "If you'll follow me, I'll show you what we're doing."

Betty stopped at the first door on the left. She opened it, revealing a sitting area with a white couch and matching wing backed chair. By the far window sat a desk with a laptop, still in its box. A bookshelf was lined with medical books and titles about Christian living.

"This will be your sister, Sarah's room," she said, walking through the room and opening the far door. Maxine and Robin looked past her to see a four poster bed with plastic wrapped mattresses, two wing back chairs sitting in the middle of the room, and a carpet rolled up, propped against a wall. A fireplace with a white marble mantle occupied the center of the farthest wall from the door. "She has an appointment with me after classes tomorrow to finalize colors," she said, shutting the door and gesturing with her hand. "That door leads to the bathroom, and that one to the dressing room." They left the room and crossed the hall. "This is Tony's office," she said. "I'm to redesign it and rearrange it to accommodate another desk, and make the decor a little more feminine."

Robin poked her head into the office and saw a huge oak desk with just a black blotter on top of it. A wooden filing cabinet sat behind the desk. A dark brown leather couch sat in the center of the room, and floor to ceiling bookshelves lined every wall. The single room was easily bigger than Robin's entire apartment.

Betty gestured down the hall. "I'll show you Derrick's room now. I've had painters here since Tony called me at ten this morning. I'm so thankful we were able to get someone in with absolutely no notice on a Thursday afternoon."

She took Robin and Maxine back into the hall to another room. This one had an open door. As soon as they got close to the door, the smell of fresh interior latex paint immediately wafted out. Robin could see through the open doorway beyond the sitting room. Plastic drop cloths covered the carpet and two men in coveralls rolled navy colored paint onto the trimmed walls with professional precision.

"Do you have furniture coming?" Maxine asked.

Betty answered. "Yes. At four today. I have a black leather couch coming for this room, and an oak desk and bookshelf. The bedroom is going to be white and with navy trim. I would have dearly loved to have done a wash but there really isn't time."

"That sounds great," Maxine said. "What are these walls going to be below the chair rail?"

"I'm thinking gray, with nautical paintings above and a matching gray mat inside oak frames."

Maxine nodded. "I can supply the artwork if you can get it framed and matted."

"She absolutely can," Robin said. Maxine's artistic eye that helped her excel in the advertising industry had also developed her into a stellar painter in her own right. "Wait until you see her work."

Betty raised an eyebrow. "Indeed. Tony had mentioned the same but I didn't want to presume. In fact, he wants me to commission you first for any of his contracts."

The three women discussed furniture, colors, and what needed to be bought until Robin's cell phone rang. She saw Tony's number and answered with a smile. "Hi, you."

"Hello, *cara*. I saw your new car in the garage and wanted to let you know we are on our way up."

Robin felt so excited at meeting Derrick she decided not to chide him about the car any more today. "I'll see you in a second." She walked through the apartment, so inspired to see the love that Tony had put into these rooms. She stepped down into the living room and crossed over to greet the elevator just as it arrived.

A young man hesitated before he stepped off, eyeing her with cautious curiosity. He wore dirty jeans and a black leather jacket with a hole in the elbow. His face was chapped red beneath scruffy, unshaven cheeks. He had black hair that was almost curly, brown eyes the color of dark caramel and pale olive skin. He looked wafer thin, nearly gaunt with sallow cheeks, as if he hadn't had many good meals in the last several weeks. Robin immediately fell in love with him. She held both of her hands out. "You must be Derrick," she said with a smile. "I'm Robin. It's so nice to meet you.

He stared at her hands before taking them. She squeezed his chapped and calloused fingers and released him just as Maxine came into the room, laughing. "This is my sister, Maxine," she said.

Maxine raised a hand in a greeting. "Hello, Derrick. It's wonderful to meet you." She fastened her jacket. "Are you ready?"

Derrick shoved his hands into his jacket pockets. "Ready for what?"

Maxine pulled her car keys out of her pocket and jingled them. "Shopping! Tony tells me you need new clothes. And, I'm just sure I need new shoes. You know the old saying about two birds?"

Robin said, "Maxi and I were just here supervising the

decorator for your bedroom. Hopefully, we covered everything." She turned to Tony who followed Derrick out of the elevator. He reached into the inside pocket of his coat and pulled out a thin wallet. He handed a black credit card to Maxine and said, "I assume you will make it up to me in paintings very soon?"

Maxine looked at the credit card and asked, "Seriously?"

Tony answered, "If you are concerned or have any issues, call my cell. I have already spoken to the bank so you should have no problems anywhere you go."

He put a hand on Derrick's elbow. With a straight face, he said, "Derrick, you are about to go shopping for clothes, shoes, other apparel, and accessories in the company of a beautiful, smart, and talented woman who has just been given a credit limit that approaches infinity. Consider this a rare opportunity—and take advantage of it—but carry everything she hands you. For the next few hours, you are basically a pack mule."

At Derrick's puzzled look, Maxine released a joyful laugh. "Let's go. I can't wait to get to know more about you."

Robin looked at her watch. "I have to run, too. I have some paperwork to do then I have to meet Craig. I'll see you tomorrow?"

He took her hand and kissed the knuckles. "Count on it, my love."

ROBIN sat at the small, shabby, round table in her worn kitchen. She could reach and open the refrigerator with one hand, and reach and touch the wall opposite the refrigerator with the other. A Formica covered breakfast bar separated the kitchen from the 'living room,' a space squeezed tight with a couch, a chair, and an old television. Down a narrow hallway were two small bedrooms, one hers and one shared by Maxine and Sarah, and a bathroom that was barely big enough for the shower stall and toilet.

She had worked two jobs for years to provide a home and an education for her sisters. She'd vowed to herself that she would do it, without help from anyone, even them, and give them the opportunity to have the kind of life that their addiction-driven mother never offered them. She would give them careers that would allow them to live independently from ever needing anything provided to them by anyone else.

Thinking back, she pulled a tin of mints out from under a stack of mail and popped one in her mouth, sucking on it as she thought of the woman who had given birth to her. Their mother had been driven by her addictions—mastered by them really, enslaved to them—and never seemed to care one way or the other what that meant to her three daughters. Robin had cared for her younger sisters as well as possible, protecting them, doing her best to handle daily needs. But their lives had been the stuff of nightmares filled with hunger, fear, pain, and desperation.

The murder of their mother and her last boyfriend had released the girls from one nightmare, only to introduce the older two to another. From the time she could walk, it felt like Robin had scraped and scratched for survival and she so desperately wanted to make sure her sisters had a solid base to break the cycle.

It felt strange, now, to think that she no longer worked alone. There was a time when she wouldn't accept help from Tony, out of stubborn pride. Then she learned that he expressed love by doing and giving, and had gradually started to accept that.

The idea that Tony would soon be her partner in life gave her a bit of pause. Especially now that planning for the wedding was suddenly upon her, she honestly didn't know what she was doing. Who was she to think she could marry a man who had to whittle the invitation list to his wedding down from over fifteen hundred people and considered doing so a hardship? Whether Tony knew it or acknowledged it or not, he was entirely ten levels above her league.

The door opened and Maxine breezed into the apartment. "That boy is going to break some hearts now that I've had my way with him," she said, shedding her coat. She threw it over the back of the couch and set her purse on the counter. "He has a natural sense of style, too. Once I explained to him the process, he took right to it. I even took him by my salon. Instead of balking at being at a women's salon, he sat there in his new clothes and just charmed Francine."

"I really like him. I can see why Tony was so drawn to him. Something about him—"

Maxine raised an eyebrow. "Okay. What's wrong?"

Robin's stared for a moment at Maxine before laughing and shaking her head. "Goodness, Maxi. I can't hide anything from you, can I?"

"What, Robin? What happened?"

"Nothing—" She looked at her phone again. "It's just that a homemaking magazine just called me for an interview. That makes three magazines and four newspapers since Monday."

"So give the interviews." Maxine set a shopping bag

full of shoes on the floor by the couch. "I think it's awesome. Oh! Do them at Hank's Place! Get that name recognition out there."

"I don't know how to give an interview. I've never given an interview in my life."

"Then call Tony. I'm sure he has some PR department to handle this kind of thing. He is very careful with his public image."

"Maxi." Her breath came out in a sigh. She slowly stood from the table. "What am I doing? I feel like I'm playing a game and any minute now someone is going to unmask me and everyone will know how I am absolutely the wrong woman to be marrying that man."

Maxine came toward her and put her hands on her shoulders. "Listen to me. You will never find anyone who loves you as much as that man does. You have a jewel in him. You are blessed. Don't foolishly toss it aside because you can't see beyond his material possessions."

"Can anyone see past his material possessions?" She looked at her watch. "I have to run. I'm meeting Craig at the restaurant."

"Hey," Maxine said as Robin started to dash down the hallway. "Be careful with that."

Robin smiled and dismissively waved her hand. "It's fine."

CHEF Casey stood behind the big stainless steel island next to a nervous assistant who deftly cut carrots into julienne strips. He looked up as Robin walked into the room. He gave her the grimace that passed for his smile, making his uneven teeth flash startling white against his ebony face. "Hiya."

Robin smiled back, "Hiya yourself." She stepped aside and encouraged Craig Bartlett to step forward.

Casey looked with curiosity at Robin's guest, but continued their ritual greeting with, "All right, then."

"Casey, I'd like you to meet my father, Craig Bartlett." Robin still felt strange saying that. Craig's feet shuffled and he nervously nodded at Casey, but he did not speak. He stood well over six feet tall, with dirty blond hair and pale blue eyes. His plaid shirt stretched tight over a broad chest and large stomach.

The old chef left his assistant and came around the table. When he reached Craig, he held out his hand. "Pleasure," he said.

Craig took the thin chef's offered hand and shook it with a mumbled, "Nice to meet you."

Casey squinted his eyes. "Seen you around here. Recognize the face. Used to stay here late nights Robin tended bar."

It was nearly the longest speech Robin had ever heard Casey utter. And it told her that Casey knew that Craig was a recovering alcoholic. She had no idea what else he might already know.

The men shook hands and Robin spoke, "I told Craig you might be able to put him to work."

"That right? What can ya do, Craig?" The much shorter and bonier old man asked, his voice skeptical yet open.

Craig ran his finger under the collar of his new shirt. "The truth is I ain't never worked an honest day in my life. So, I don't know. I'll do whatever you tell me to do."

"Eh?" Casey's eyes shifted to Robin.

Knowing her friend's protective feelings toward her, Robin put her hand on her father's arm to convey her support of him. "Craig just came out of rehab. He has a court date in five months, after which he'll very probably go back to prison. In the meantime, he needs some kind of work."

"I can wash dishes, if you want." Craig offered, looking at the industrial washing station.

Casey stepped back and looked him up and down. "You's big. Look strong. You'll do." Robin smiled, relieved. Casey continued. "Need to get you into a uniform. For now, fetch one o' them aprons over there. But listen up. This is my kitchen. Do what I say how I say when I say or you's out. Don't care if your little girl is the boss. Nobody messes in my kitchen. Clear?"

Craig nodded. "Much obliged. I understand."

Robin left the men and moved through the kitchen and down the hall to her office. She opened it and slipped in, shutting it behind her and leaning against it. Her hands shook and she pressed them to her eyes.

She didn't know why she suddenly felt so overwhelmed. Six months ago, she was exhausted physically, and shut down emotionally. Working six days a week, she bartended at one job and waited tables at another. All that mattered to her then was getting Sarah through college and making sure both of her sisters had the means to support themselves so that they would never have to rely on anyone else for anything.

She didn't know God, then. She didn't know Tony, then. She had no idea that she served drinks to her own father every single night when she worked at the bar—a father who now faced sentencing in just a few short months for a fifteen year old manslaughter charge from when, years ago, he stepped out of prison, dug up his pistol, and shot and killed Robin's mother and her mother's male companion.

Now her mind reeled on how different things were, how much better. She slid down the door and wrapped her arms around her legs, whispering a tearful prayer of thanks to God for not turning His back on her, even when she didn't know He existed. While she had His attention, she put in a plea, begging him to help her with this looming fear of not being the right Mrs. Viscolli for Tony.

CHAPTER FOUR

Tony sat on the worn plaid couch in the living room of Peter and Caroline O'Farrell. Peter, Tony's mentor and dear friend, headed up the extensive children and youth department at Boston Central Bible Church. Next to Tony on the couch sat a little girl of Chinese descent with straight black hair and a crooked smile. Angel Dove, as Caroline named her, had no idea how she got there or where she came from.

Caroline had first found her digging through the church's soup kitchen Dumpster after lunch was served one afternoon two years ago. The doctor guessed her age at the time at about six. Angel Dove, currently the youngest child in the O'Farrell home, was at the time directing Tony which color of crayon to shade the puff of smoke coming off of the cartoon train in the coloring book in his lap.

Derrick and Peter had braved the winter storm to walk to the corner store so they could replenish the spent supply of milk the children would need with dinner. Robin and Caroline busied themselves in the kitchen. That meant that

Tony and Angel Dove had a few moments of quiet time.

Looking at her sent Tony back a number of years in his memory. He remembered the first time Peter brought him here to this house, the very night he'd given his life to Christ. Peter's wife, Caroline, had greeted him warmly, with the first hug he'd had in his life. He remembered nearly being brought to tears by that embrace.

Like Angel Dove, the O'Farrell's had taken Tony in and fostered him, teaching him about life and God the Father, Jesus the Son, and the Holy Spirit. He had learned, grown, and learned some more. He cherished his relationship with these two amazing people. While Peter and Caroline taught him the love of a family, he used the extensive library at the huge inner city church to feed his hungry soul with the Word of God.

By the end of the year, he had saved every dime he earned as one of the church's janitorial crew and invested it. With the profit from his initial investment, he made another one, and another one. Now he was what the press labeled "Boston royalty," an entrepreneur who dabbled in just about anything, all the while pouring money into church ministries and local charities.

Never having children of their own, the O'Farrells fostered dozens over the years. Caroline never turned a child away, even if she had to make a pallet on the floor of a bedroom while she found a better home. Tony shared a room with three other boys the year he lived with them. Today, he financed a network of children's homes throughout the country.

"I have sandwiches," Caroline said, bringing Tony back to the present. She set a huge platter of peanut butter and jelly sandwiches next to two bowls of potato chips. Bright red tendrils of hair escaped the pony tail on the top of her head.

Tony glanced up to find Robin strolling out of the kitchen carrying a pitcher of lemonade. She gave him a warm smile that thrilled him. He so enjoyed seeing how well his bride to be fit so perfectly into his life and felt so comfortable with the people who meant the most to him.

"Yummy!" Angel said as she hopped off the couch and ran to the table.

Caroline smiled and put her hand on the head of her daughter. As they stood to go to the table, Tony slipped an arm around Robin's waist and said, "We are so honored that you and Peter are going to stand up with us at our wedding. We were hoping that Angel Dove could serve as our flower girl."

"Oh, I bet she would love it," Caroline said, walking forward to hug Robin first, then Tony.

In what seemed like incredible timing, the second youngest child and youngest boy in the O'Farrell home appeared from the kitchen carrying a stack of plates to the table. Little did he know he was about to become the topic of conversation.

"There's more," Robin said. "We would also be honored if Isaac would be our ring bearer. I know he's a little old, but—"

"What do you say, lad? Do you want to be in Uncle Tony's wedding?"

The little tawny haired boy with the round glasses scrunched his eight-year-old face up. "Do I have to dress up in a monkey suit?"

Caroline's laughter rang out through the room. "Aye, you do. And you'll look sharp in it, too. Like James Bond." She waved at the table. "Now, eat. Get as much as you want. I can make more."

The back door opened and Peter and Derrick came in, stomping the snow off their feet. Peter pulled his glasses from his face when they steamed up in the heat and Derrick shed his new ski coat. "It is really coming down out there." Peter set a gallon of milk on the table. "There's your milk, my dear."

"Thank you, love," Caroline said, taking the milk into the kitchen.

"Temperature is dropping," Derrick said. He grabbed half a sandwich from the platter and ate it in two bites. Caroline came back into the room carrying a glass of milk which she handed Derrick.

"We should probably go, then," Tony said. He grabbed Robin's coat that she'd hung on the back of a chair and held it out for her to slip her arms into it. "I still need to get Robin home."

"Can I drive?" Derrick asked. He drained the milk in a few long swallows and grabbed another sandwich.

"If the weather wasn't so nasty, I'd say yes."

"I have to learn how to drive in the snow sometime," Derrick said.

"He has a point," Peter said, pulling the ski cap off of his salt and pepper hair.

Tony nodded. "You're right. After we drop Robin off, maybe I'll let you drive. Let me see how bad the roads are."

Derrick let out a loud, "Whoop," and went rushing outside, yelling good-bye to Caroline as he went.

Caroline laughed and put her hand to her chest. "You make me proud, Tony," she said. "What you're doing for that young man is a good thing."

Tony nodded, looking at the door from which Derrick had gone out. "He seems like a fine boy. Ever since he came to me last Wednesday, he's just gratefully accepted what I've offered. I don't know if he's waiting for a catch, casing me, or just plain happy to be out."

Peter put his glasses back on. "I'm guessing the last," he said. "I've met a lot of lost boys. You can tell when they're sincere and when they're just biding their time. He will be a great man one day, if he lets God use him."

"I agree." Tony buttoned his coat. "Ready to traverse the roads, *cara*?"

"I guess," she said. "We probably should leave before it gets worse." She stepped forward and hugged Caroline. "Thank you. I enjoyed the movie and time with you."

"I enjoyed it as well, love. I shall see you at church tomorrow."

Tony stepped outside and the wind immediately drove snow into his face. He held up his arm to block the icy blast and took Robin's arm in his other hand. "Be careful," he yelled against the wind. "The walk will be slippery."

He walked carefully along the sidewalk to the gate. The latch was frozen shut. Derrick kicked it with a booted foot and it shook loose so that Tony could open it. They reached his car, parked on the curb, and piled in, Robin in the front seat next to Tony, Derrick in the back.

Tony started the car and cold air blasted out from the vents. "It will warm up in a sec," he said when Robin shivered. As he spoke, the air started to feel warmer.

He put the car in drive and realized after just a few yards that he would not be able to see in the driving snow. He stopped at an intersection. "We're going to have to take the Charlie," he said. "I can't drive in this."

Robin shivered and looked at her feet. She'd worn canvas shoes, not knowing that the weather would turn. "I don't have a Charlie stop close to me," she said.

"Well…" He thought about the available options.

"You'll just have to stay at my place. I have a stop right near me."

Just then, Robin's phone rang. Tony saw Sarah's picture on the screen as Robin answered it. "Hey, Sarah," she said. Tony inched the car forward carefully. "Slow down," Robin said. "I can't understand you."

Tony turned off of the street that housed the pastors of Boston Central Bible and pulled into the church parking lot, driving through the empty lot to the end. He parked in a spot closest to the entrance to the subway system, but did not turn the car off yet.

"Well, that's okay," she said. "I'm stuck, too, and am just going to go to Tony's. Take the Charlie to Tony's apartment. The two of us can just stay in your room tonight. Your bed's set up, and you have a couch in there, too." Tony nodded and Robin finished the call. "You know which stop to take? Oh, that's right. You met the decorator there. Okay. Good. I'll see you as soon as you get there." She hung up and turned her head to him. "She's been working at the hospital. There's no way she can drive home, either."

"It's just two stops up from my place," he said. "I'll call the guard in case she beats us there." While he placed the call, he realized that ninety percent of him was thankful Sarah would be spending the night as well. But he also admitted that there was that ten percent that fought the constant temptation of knowing that Robin would certainly be his wife, so why continue to deny themselves the fulfillment of pushing their physical relationship forward? Knowing she was sleeping in his apartment, he didn't know if he had the strength to battle that. Sarah's arrival was certainly an answer to prayer.

"This," he said before turning off the car and waving at

the falling driven snow outside, "this is why I live in Florida in the winter."

He looked over his shoulder at Derrick, who was adjusting his hat. "That's a good idea, man. Let's go to Florida."

Tony laughed. "I think we will. We can leave Tuesday. I think a week or two will warm our bones nicely."

Derrick stopped moving. "Seriously?"

"Of course. I have a ton of work waiting for me down there, so it will be good to go. You'll like my house there. It's right on the beach with a pool. You can vacation before starting your new job at the hotel."

Robin glared at him before her face cracked a smile and laughter bubbled past the feigned seriousness. "You're just mean."

"One day soon, *cara*, you will be free to come and go with me as well. I look forward to it." He put his hand on the door handle. "Ready?"

ROBIN met the elevator, relieved to see Sarah step off. "I've been worried!" She said, hugging her sister.

"I missed the train and had to wait for the next one," Sarah said, pulling her coat off and hanging it on the stand next to the door. She held up her overnight bag. "It was a long wait and my phone died right when we hung up. I'd planned on going to mom and dad's tonight, thankfully, so I have a bag packed."

"Did you find someone to take your Sunday School class?"

"Yep. All set. I'll just go with you in the morning since we can ride the train."

Robin's phone rang in her hand. "Hey Maxi. She just got here." Sarah rolled her eyes at her older sister's display of what she considered over- protectiveness. She made a drinking motion with her hand and headed toward the kitchen

On the other end, Maxine said. "Okay, good. Glad you're all safe. If the roads are clear, I'll bring you clothes in the morning. If not, I'll see you at church."

Robin disconnected the call and stepped down into the living room. She gestured at the doorway toward the kitchen. "I guess I should have warned her Derrick was in there."

"I guess she'll find out soon enough," Tony said, typing on his phone. "Did you get settled into Sarah's room okay?"

Robin curled up on the couch next to him. "I did. I'm so glad you're not thousands of miles away and that we were together tonight. She would have been stuck."

Tony put his arm around her and kissed her forehead. "This will be her home, too. You two will soon think of it that way. You could have come here whether I was home or not."

Robin linked her fingers with his, pulling his arm closer around her. "We could go ahead and skip this whole event of the year, thing, and just get married. Then I could move in now."

"You're not getting out of it that easy," he said, setting his phone on the couch next to him. "But, nice try, to tempt me like that."

She smiled up at him and stared into his eyes. "Tempted, eh?"

His smile faded and his eyes grew serious. Robin felt her heart rate accelerate. "Like you wouldn't believe," he admitted softly, running a finger down her cheek.

"Disgusting!" Sarah said, storming into the room.

Tony frowned and lifted his head. Robin settled more comfortably against him. "I beg your pardon?" she asked.

Sarah pointed in the general direction of the kitchen. "That boy in there is disgusting. And crude."

The dining room door swung open, and Derrick came through, wearing cotton pajama pants and a white T-shirt, holding a large tuna fish sandwich in one hand and a big glass of chocolate milk in the other. "You want to watch the game?" He asked Tony as he sat on the couch next to Robin.

"Sure," Tony said. He gestured at the coffee table. "The television remote is the black one."

"Seriously?" Sarah said, crossing her arms. "You're just going to let him eat that in here?"

"I wasn't rude. I offered her some," Derrick said around a bite of tuna. He chewed and swallowed. "But she *certainly* did *not* want any." He emphasized certainly and not to sound haughty.

Robin giggled and Sarah rolled her eyes. "I'm going to bed. I've had a long day. Goodnight."

ROBIN opened the door to Sarah's room and stopped short when she found her on the couch, reading a book. "Hey," she said, coming all the way into the room and sitting next to her, setting the T-shirt and shorts Tony had loaned her on the cushion next to her. "I thought you were tired an hour ago."

"I wasn't, but I just didn't want to stay in there with him and watch that silly basketball show."

Robin raised an eyebrow. "With Tony?"

Sarah sighed. "Of course not. I love Tony."

"So, Derrick then?"

"Yeah. Something about him irritates me. Maybe it's just the smell of that canned fish he's devouring." Sarah's eyebrows scrunched down behind her glasses, clearly perturbed.

"You must have just gotten off on the wrong foot. He's really nice."

Sarah put her book down and took off her glasses, then stretched. "I'll take your word for it." She looked around at the big, nicely furnished room. "It's crazy to think that this will be our home soon, isn't it?"

Robin nodded. "I'm having a hard time coming to grips with it myself. I don't know how it happened."

Sarah leaned over and hugged her. "Because you're wonderful and you deserve happiness a thousand times over."

"I don't deserve anything more than anyone else." Robin put her hands on the side of her head. "Look at this place. Your bedroom suite is the size of our entire apartment. How do I be a wife in this home?"

"You just learn how." Sarah frowned. "I'm not sure what you mean."

"It feels so right with Tony when we're at the O'Farrell's house or our apartment. Nothing seems out of place." Robin waved her hand. "It's okay. I'm just stressing out loud. Don't worry about it."

"If you're sure. I know that weddings are extremely stressful, even when you're not marrying Boston royalty. It will get better, I just know it. You and Tony were meant to be." Sarah stood. "I'm going to go to bed for real this time. Are you sleeping out here or in there with me?"

"With you, if you don't mind."

"Of course I don't mind."

Robin felt a pang of remembrance. "You used to sleep with me all the time," she said, running her hand over her sister's curly hair. "I was six when you came home from the hospital. But, you didn't have a bed, so Maxi slept on the floor and you slept next to me. Your dad would always kiss you on the forehead. I remember him. I remember he was really nice. He was just kind of, you know, not very smart I guess. I remember I'd get up at night and feed you and he would come in and sing heavy metal songs like lullabies."

Sarah's eyes filled with tears. "I wish I could remember."

Robin felt a cold shudder go through her. "No, you don't. You don't ever want to remember."

CHAPTER FIVE

Maxine opened the double door refrigerator and found the platter of sandwiches Tony said she would find there. Underneath, she found a container of potato salad and another one of cole slaw.

"Did you find everything, Maxi?" Robin asked, coming in behind her.

"I think so. If you'll put the coffee on, I'll set this out on the table."

Maxine carried the large platter through the kitchen door and into the dining room. She arranged the platter on the end of the long, long table but left the plastic wrap on it. When she went back into the kitchen, Robin was just pressing the button to start the coffee machine.

"I'm going to go ask Tony where to find plates and such," Robin said. "I don't know if he wanted to use real things or if he had paper plates somewhere."

"I'll get these salads into something other than deli containers." Maxine started opening cupboard doors. "Assuming I don't get lost in this massive edifice searching for bowls."

The door shut on Robin's laugh. Maxine kept searching. She finally opened a door and found a walk-in supply closet filled with serving platters, serving dishes, and serving bowls. Drawers revealed silverware—real silver—with a "V" engraved on the handles. On the shelf, she discovered two small glass bowls that would perfectly present the deli salads.

When Maxine went back into the kitchen, she stopped short upon seeing Barry at the sink, filling a cup with hot water. "Hi there, big guy," she greeted, hoping her lipstick was still on straight. She hadn't checked it since she left for church that morning.

"Hi, yourself," Barry said, giving her a quick glance. "Glad to see you in church this morning. I was worried the weather would keep everyone away."

She wore a plum colored knee-length skirt that perfectly matched her three-inch plum colored heels. She liked the fact that she still had to look up at him even with her three-inch boost. At her height, she considered it a rare treat to stand shorter than a man. "The streets were clear by the time I headed out. I brought Robin's new car. This way, I can take Sarah back to her car at the hospital and drive Robin home."

Barry nodded. "Sounds like a good plan. Is there anything I can help you with in here, Maxine?"

She raised an eyebrow. "Oh, no. I think I got it under control. And, it's Maxi, please. I've always hated Maxine. Thankfully, only Robin still sometimes calls me that." Although, she really liked hearing Barry "The Bear" say it.

Barry raised an eyebrow in his incredibly handsome face and what she could only call a teasing and somewhat mischievous grin appeared there. "Why have you always hated your name, Maxine?"

"It just doesn't suit me. I look more like a 'Stands with a Fist' than a Maxine."

Barry didn't even grin at her teasing tone. He opened a tea bag, steeped it into hot water, and set his cup out on the counter. Then put his hands in his pockets and leaned against the sink. Using a tone that teachers use when they are hopeful their students already know the answer, he asked, "You know where the name Maxine comes from?"

"Of course," Maxi nodded. "My drug addicted mother's addled brain."

Barry shook his head. "Emperor Maximus…"

"Ooh." Maxi interrupted. "Emperor! So feminine!"

Barry smiled a little bit at her silliness. "He stood over eight feet tall. It's from his name that we get the word maximum. And the term maximal. And the name Maxine." With a half grin and a teasing tone meant to hook her heart, he announced, "Your name basically means you're… the most."

Maxine cocked her head and slitted her eyes. "Really? No kidding?"

With an exaggerated motion that really turned out to look quite large considering his stature, Barry crossed his heart with his finger. For the moment, she managed to ignore the wedding ring on his left hand. "Hope to die if it's a lie."

She looked at him as if she remained unconvinced. "How did you know that?"

Barry's grin transformed into a smug smile, "I went to law school, Maxine. I know things."

She threw her head back and laughed. "I see. Apparently they taught you humility, there, too."

"Humility? Oh, absolutely." Barry nodded and sipped

his tea.

The door opened and Robin came in. "Hi, Barry," she said, going to the refrigerator. "I didn't see Jacqui this morning."

His lips thinned. "She is not really a regular church attendee. She usually has other plans."

Robin's hands paused. "Oh. Okay. Sorry to bring it up."

"No need to apologize. It is what it is." He lifted his cup as if in a toast. "Ladies. Thank you for putting out lunch. Tony said he wants to make this a regular Sunday thing now that he will have a family here."

"I think that's awesome," Maxine said, "provided he allows me to find a television with a game on it."

Barry put his hand to his heart. "I will ensure that I, I mean you, have access to televised sporting events." He laughed. "See what I must sacrifice for my friends?"

Robin looked between the two of them. "I'm sure Tony won't mind you turning on the television. I bet Derrick would join you in watching, too."

"I'll go see what I can do." Barry left the room and Maxine went back to scooping potato salad into a bowl.

"What's going on, Maxine?" Robin grabbed a spoon and emptied the cole slaw into the bowl.

"What do you mean?"

"Don't be coy. I know you."

Maxine tossed the empty container into the sink. "I'm not meaning to flirt. He's just so handsome and so—"

"Married?"

Maxine sighed. "You're right." She picked up her bowl. "I know you're right. I'll let up."

Robin put a hand on Maxine's arm, "Was he flirting back?"

Maxine looked as if she could answer differently. Instead, she answered honestly. "Not even a little bit."

Before Robin could chide her any further, Maxine pushed through the kitchen door and set the salad next to the tray of sandwiches.

ROBIN spun around and Maxine catcalled at her. "Gorgeous, sister."

Sarah sat on her knees backwards on the couch, propping her elbow on the back of the couch and resting her chin in her hand. "You look wonderful!"

Robin ran her hand down the side of the red dress. It crisscrossed over the front and tied together at the hip. It fell to her knees, and she wore a pair of two-inch red heels Maxine had talked her into buying. She had to keep herself from tugging at the bodice, worried that the dress's design revealed too much cleavage.

"I don't know. Maybe it's too much," she said, turning to go back to her room. "I have a sweater dress I bought for Sundays."

A knock sounded at the door and Maxine rushed to answer it. "Don't you dare," she said. "You leave that on. Besides, he's here, now."

Robin heard Tony speak. "Hello, Maxine. *Buon San Valentino.*"

Maxine laughed and opened the door wider. "If you just said Happy Valentine's Day, then the same to you. Welcome back from the sunshine state."

Tony stepped into view. "Thank you. I thought I would have to drag Derrick back—" He stopped speaking when he saw Robin. His eyes widened and his mouth gaped open.

Robin took a step back and tugged at the dress. "I should probably put on a different dress," she said nervously.

"No!" All three people said at the same time.

The look on Tony's face made Robin's breath catch. She wasn't sure he was even breathing. She could see the pulse racing at his neck. He looked nearly angry, but that wasn't right. Just really intense. Very, very intense. After a heartbeat or two, Tony stepped toward her and took her hand. "No, please." he said more gently. "You look amazing. *Magnifica*. I am so proud that you will be my wife." He brushed at his black sleeve. "I am also glad I told Maxine I was wearing a tuxedo so that she would know how to advise you to dress."

Robin laughed and gathered her black shawl. "You know us too well."

Maxine held up her hand. "Have fun kids. Don't do anything I wouldn't do."

The door shut on Sarah saying, "Maxi!"

"I missed you. I'm glad you're home." Robin hooked her arm through Tony's. "I've never been out on Valentine's Day before, though I've worked plenty."

Tony put his hand on top of hers on his arm as they walked down the stairs to the parking lot. His limousine driver stood ready and opened the door as they approached, closing it quickly behind them. Robin settled back next to Tony against the soft leather seats. He rarely used the limo, and she was curious about what the evening would bring.

"Margaret got the final list of guests' names to Stephanie yesterday," Tony said as the car pulled into the late afternoon traffic.

"I know. They have both been texting me like mad. I have an appointment with Stephanie a week from Wednesday to look at flowers and place settings for the tables."

Tony linked his fingers with hers. "Have you selected your wedding dress yet?"

Robin sighed, mind whirling with details. "That's next Tuesday. I looked through magazines with Maxi and Sarah for hours and hours. We found four possibilities and sent them to the dress shop. I go try them on in a week. Whenever we get that dress figured out, Maxi said we'll be able to get their dresses. I guess there's something stylistic about that. Or something."

Tony laughed and brought her hand up to his lips, kissing the back of it. "Is it so terrible?"

She leaned forward and put her hand on his cheek. "No. Knowing how much you'll love it is making it bearable. But it's new territory and I'm well beyond out of my comfort zone."

"Just think about how easy planning a dinner party will be after this," he said. She opened her mouth to protest, but he covered her mouth with his own, drowning out the sound. Robin quit thinking about wedding colors and details and design and styles and just lost herself in the feel of him, the smell, the taste. Her head spun and her heart beat a frantic rhythm as the car shot through the streets of the city.

She barely felt them slowing down and stopping until Tony lifted his head. The inside of the car felt hot, and she fanned her face as she put a hand to the intricate "updo" Maxine had twisted out of her hair, making sure all strands were in place. The car started forward again, and she looked out the window and saw that they'd pulled into a small airport not far from Logan.

The car stopped next to Tony's Gulfstream. A pilot stood next to the open door and waved as they got out of the car. Tony took Robin's hand and walked toward the stairs leading into the jet. "Good afternoon, Jeremy," he said, shaking the pilot's hand.

"Mr. Viscolli. Happy Valentine's Day, Miss Bartlett. We have clear skies all night long."

"Wonderful." Tony gestured to the stairs. "After you, *cara*."

Curious now about where they might be going, Robin precariously climbed the stairs in her high heels. She ducked her head as she entered the cabin, remembering the white leather couch, white leather chairs, and the shiny mahogany tables from her trip to Florida at Christmas.

Choosing a chair next to a window for takeoff, she sat and buckled up. The only other time she'd flown anywhere in her life had been her recent trip to and from Florida in this same aircraft. Knowing how much Tony traveled, she knew she had better get used to it. But the thought of the little jet thousands of feet in the air made her stomach do a small flip.

Tony sat next to her and put a hand on her knee. "Relax," he said, "Jeremy is the best there is."

"You would have the best," she smiled, trying and failing to relax. "Are you going to tell me where we're going?"

He raised an eyebrow. "I told you. Dinner."

"Dinner requires an airplane?"

"For Valentine's Day? I should think so." He reached a hand into his jacket pocket as the plane taxied away, pulling out a long thin box wrapped in a red ribbon. "For you, my love. Because you have stolen my heart."

"Tony," Robin said, pleased and annoyed at the same time. She took the box and slipped off the ribbon. When she opened the lid, she gasped. Suspended from a silver chain was a heart framed out in diamonds. That heart was stacked on top of and slightly over top of a heart crusted with about a hundred small perfectly cut rubies. As she lifted it out of the box, she saw a card inside with a Bible verse written on it. It said: *Who can find a virtuous wife? For her worth is far above rubies. The heart of her husband safely trusts her; so he will have no lack of gain. Proverbs 31:10-11*

"Do you like it?" Tony asked, taking the necklace from her to slip it around her neck, reaching around her to fasten it. "I think it's perfect for this dress."

Robin brushed her fingers over the hearts. "I don't..."

Tony sighed. "I know. You don't want jewelry from me. Etcetera. Do you like it, *cara*?"

With a smile, Robin leaned forward and kissed him. "Yes. Very much. Thank you."

"*Bene.*" He kissed her again as the plane's wheels left the ground.

ROBIN recognized the New York City skyline. She grinned and she clutched Tony's hand as the jet landed on a small airstrip just across the river. They stepped off the plane and were ushered to a waiting helicopter. Robin could not believe the thrill she felt as the helicopter took off and flew over the Hudson toward the city.

Tony put his arm around her and in the light of the setting sun pointed out land marks and places of interest. She didn't think she quit smiling the entire flight.

It felt like no sooner had they lifted off than the

helicopter landed on the roof of a building. In just minutes she had seen the mighty Hudson River, the Statue of Liberty, and a collection of some of the tallest buildings in the world. It felt exhilarating. Robin thought she could have easily spent the entire evening just sightseeing the city from on high. But her stomach growled as they walked across the roof.

As the helicopter lifted away, it became just the two of them again. Robin wrapped her shawl tighter around her shoulders and kept her hand securely in Tony's. A uniformed guard met them at the door of the roof and opened it for them. Robin recognized the scrolling 'V' of the Viscolli emblem on his emerald green jacket.

As they entered the warm interior, she inquired, "Where are we?"

"A little restaurant I own," Tony answered with a smile. "I hope you're hungry. The chef here is the best in this amazing city. People have reservations for tonight going back to last year."

Another uniformed employee met them at the elevator. "Mr. Viscolli," he said in a smooth and cultured voice. "How was your trip?"

"We had a nice flight, Zach." Tony gestured and had Robin precede him into the elevator.

They rode the elevator down one flight. It opened onto the reception area of the restaurant. Robin stepped out and felt her feet sink into plush carpet. Emerald green, shiny brass, black marble—the entrance was absolutely beautiful. A hostess in a classy Viscolli uniform walked toward them through the crowd of hopeful patrons patiently waiting for their tables. "Mr. Viscolli," she greeted, her white teeth shining against her dark face, "it is such an honor to have you here with us tonight. Miss Bartlett, I'm so pleased you could join us. If you'll follow me, your table is ready."

They left the waiting area and entered the dining room. Robin avoided fiddling with the necklace while they approached a table for two nestled beside the huge window overlooking the amazing city. The table was covered with a cream colored cloth and in the center sat a gold vase with a single red rose. Robin sat in a plush chair with gold and cream brocade fabric.

As they took their seats, the hostess said, "This is Luke. He will be serving you tonight." She gestured at a waiter who approached just as Tony sat.

"Mr. Viscolli, it is an honor to serve you." The young man looked to be about Sarah's age. He was short, thin, with dark black hair and a long nose.

"Drew the short straw, did you Luke?" Tony teased.

Luke directed his attention to Tony and, perfectly poised with a sincere smile, answered, "Hardly, sir. I've looked forward to this since you made your reservation and I will give you my very best. Would you care to see the menu, or do you know what you'd like to order this evening?"

Tony held his palm up in a questioning manner to Robin, who knew what he asked by the gesture. "Go ahead," she said, "you know what I like."

She barely listened to Tony order as she watched the sun set and the lights come on in the buildings around them. The Empire State building several blocks away suddenly lit up the inside windows in the shape of a gigantic heart. When the waiter left, she leaned forward and took his hand. "This is magical. Thank you."

Tony ran his thumb over the sapphire on her finger. "I am glad you are pleased. I have been looking forward to this date. I planned it while Derrick and I were in Florida."

"How's it going with Derrick?"

"It's going well. I think getting away with him and removing him from the city for a couple of weeks was the best thing to do. He was trying very hard to hide it, but he was going through withdrawal."

"I'm sure the sun and surf helped with that."

"More than you or I know. We also had a lot of down time to talk. I shared the Gospel with him, and my testimony. He is starting to trust me a little more. I don't think he believes we're quite for real yet, though."

"He starts work at the hotel tomorrow, right?"

"Yes. And night school next week." Tony released her hand and straightened as Luke arrived with their drinks and the hors d'oeuvre of bruschetta topped with tomatoes and Italian herbs as the first course of the seven courses he'd ordered. As soon as they were both served, Tony took her hand again. "Let us give thanks for this meal and the traveling mercies with which God has blessed us."

CHAPTER SIX

The meal would go down as one of the finest she had ever eaten and she felt warm and full. After dessert and coffee, Robin followed Tony through the halls of the restaurant, passing by the huge kitchen, and into a small office. It was very similar to her office at Hank's Place. A tall man with a white chef's hat and a chocolate stained apron waited there for them. He had black hair and a close cropped black goatee. Every aspect of his uniform looked professional from his hat to his pants except that he wore a pair of purple high top sneakers with electric orange laces.

"Robin, I'd like to introduce to you Marcus Williams. Marcus is the head pastry chef here at the Viscolli New York, and the supervising pastry chef for all of the Viscolli restaurants around the world."

Marcus humbly shook her hand. "It is such a pleasure, Miss Bartlett."

It suddenly struck her. "I've seen your name on e-mails at Hank's Place."

Marcus smiled, "Chef Casey is a man after my own heart. I'm trying to get free to make a visit and see if I can assist with menu updates."

"I can't wait," Robin enthused. "That mousse I just had was probably the most amazing thing I've ever tasted."

He put a hand to his heart. "You encourage me greatly."

Tony interjected, quietly saying as if in an aside, "Marcus has gallantly volunteered to take on the very daunting task of creating our wedding cake. He has already come up with some preliminary plans. I will give you the drawings, but I wanted you two to meet in person."

Robin was very interested. "Thank you. I cannot wait to see what you came up with. How long will it take?"

"My team will arrive the first of April. The Boston hotel kitchen will accommodate us for the cake baking and decorating. Not having to transport everything to the site will make it much easier. We will do all of the flowers, gum paste, and sugar sculptures immediately and let them begin to set."

Eyes wide, she said, "It will take you three weeks to do the cake?"

"Oh yes. I would prefer five, but I have other commitments, unfortunately."

Tony made a clicking sound with his tongue, "The Camp David thing in March."

Marcus nodded exactly once. "Don't worry, sir. I'll be done with that in plenty of time."

Tony half grinned. "I'm not worried. You'll make us proud."

And it struck Robin, in that heart beat, that "the Camp David thing" when translated into English meant, "That cake Marcus Williams must set before the President of these United States, the First Lady, and, no doubt, select dignitaries." This man put a higher priority on *her* wedding cake than on preparing a dessert for the leader of the free world.

Marcus looked at his watch. "I must return to the kitchen. I look forward to working with you, Miss Bartlett. Mr. Viscolli knows how to contact me if you have any specific requests or instructions."

Marcus left them alone in the office and Robin spun in a circle. "Okay, I have to ask."

Tony cut her off, "What's with the shoes?"

"What's with the shoes?" She confirmed.

"I should have told you about that in advance. I apologize." Tony put his hand in the small of her back and his voice became almost solemn. "Some time ago, Marcus had a first cousin named Nick Williams. They were very close. Nick, fresh out of high school, joined the armed forces shortly after this great city fell under attack. Unfortunately, Nick was killed in action a few years later. There's a much longer story about the style and choice of colors, but the bottom line is that Marcus wears those shoes to honor Nick and the men with whom he served."

Suddenly, the purple and orange sneakers no longer struck her as funny. "And the Camp David thing?"

Tony shook his head, "Unrelated, but interesting that Marcus was handpicked, no? He probably doesn't even prioritize it as very important. I sponsor a special youth camp each year in support of children and families of our fallen heroes. Marcus runs the kitchen for that camp every summer. I think that is where his heart really is, with those children."

"You are an amazing man, Tony Viscolli. I love you more with every waking moment."

"You are an amazing and beautiful woman, Robin Bartlett. And I can hardly wait to change your name."

Feeling a little overwhelmed, Robin decided to change the subject, "I cannot believe we will be married in two months."

Tony ran his hand down her arm. "Sixty-six days and a wake-up."

She put her hands on her cheeks. "Sixty-six days," she said. "I don't even know what to do next."

Tony pulled her into his arms. "You pick out your dress, select table settings and flowers, and keep counting down the days with me. I love you, *cara*, and our wedding will be beautiful, whatever the arrangements."

ROBIN nervously fiddled with her ring while she waited for the *Inside Boston* magazine reporter to arrive. She sat in the conference room adjacent to the office of Tony's public relations manager, Linda Cross. She still wore the clothes and makeup from the photo shoot that had taken place in a room just down the hall. She'd hoped Tony could be there for the photos, but the magazine had specifically requested only her.

The door opened and Robin's heart lurched, but Linda entered alone. She was short and stocky, with a thick waist and jet black hair. Thick glasses with square black frames dominated her face. "Don will be in momentarily," she said. "He's signing some papers for me right now." She raised an eyebrow behind her glasses. "No worries, Miss Bartlett. I'll be here the whole time."

"I've just never done this before." She licked her lips.

"A year from now, it will be old hat," Linda assured. Robin wondered if she meant that to intimidate her or make her feel more at ease, because, honestly, she wasn't feeling better in the wake of that remark.

A tap at the door preceded the entrance of Don Roberts. He was younger than Robin, tall, boy-next-door good looking with straight brown hair and a fake tan. Nothing about him made her feel at ease about this interview.

He shook her hand—again—then sat in the chair adjacent to her. He took a phone out of his pocket, pressed a series of buttons on it, then set it on the table in front of her. She could only assume he'd activated some sort of recording device. "Miss Bartlett, Robin, thank you for giving me this opportunity."

"It's my pleasure," she said around a suddenly too-dry mouth.

"Let's go ahead and cover the basics. Tell us how you met Tony."

This was the first person outside of church to address Tony as Tony and not Mr. Viscolli. It intrigued Robin. "He, ah, bought a restaurant where I worked." She cleared her throat. "We met then."

"When was that?"

"Last fall."

"And, to add a spice of romance to our story, how did he propose?"

Robin smiled and relaxed, thinking back. "Christmas Eve, on the beach in the Florida Keys."

"That's really nice," Don said. He smiled. "Tony Viscolli is a powerful force in the business world, and not just in the Boston area. He has businesses all over the country and thousands of employees. What do you think drew him to you in particular?"

Uncomfortable, Robin shrugged. "I really couldn't tell you. You'd have to ask him."

"But we can probably guess what drew you to him, right?"

Robin put her hands in her lap and laced her fingers, squeezing them tightly. "If you knew his heart, or anything about him personally, you'd not have to ask that question. He is amazing and generous and loving, and I feel so incredibly blessed."

"Is he?"

"I beg your pardon?"

"Is he really all those things? Or simply uninformed?"

Robin felt her eyebrows crease under the thick makeup from the photo shoot. "What?"

"Does he know all there is to know about you?"

Robin shifted her eyes to Linda, who frowned but did not speak. "I beg your pardon?"

Don sat forward and tapped the top of the table with every question. He looked like an anaconda eyeing a mouse. "He knows you were a waitress moonlighting as a bartender. Does he know your father went to prison for drug smuggling and now faces double murder charges? Does he know your mother was an addict who was murdered in a drug deal? Does he know you, yourself, stabbed your foster parent in the back with a buck knife? Does he know you were a fugitive until you turned eighteen and your juvenile crimes were sealed? Does he know about the improprietary manner in which you had your former employer pull strings with city hall to clear your record so you could obtain custody of one of your sisters? How did you convince that retired sailor to help you pull those strings, Miss Bartlett?"

Panic swirled in her brain, freezing her ability to form cohesive thoughts. "I don't—what are you—?" Robin gasped and looked from Don to Linda. Her heart pounded and she felt sweat break out on her forehead.

Linda pressed a button on the table next to her before standing. "Mr. Roberts? This interview is over. Our attorneys at the Anderson firm will be in contact with your editor in light of the NDA you signed and this particular line of questioning."

"You can't hide her. Believe me if I know, the tabloids know, too. This is the kind of rags to riches story that everyone will be clamoring after. You need to let her—"

As he spoke the door opened and two uniformed security officers marched into the room. They walked straight up to Don. "You need to come with us, sir," one of them said.

"Now." The other one said, picking up the reporter's phone from the table.

"Hey! You can't have that!"

"We'll return your property when you're safely outside the building, sir." The guard stepped aside, placing his body between Roberts and the two women, and gestured with his hand. "Right this way, sir."

Roberts stood but quickly bent around the guard toward Robin. "You might as well figure out the best thing to do is embrace your story and tell it, or else others will do it with their own spin and you won't be able to influence what they say."

The second guard grabbed his arm at the elbow and said, "You've already outstayed your welcome, sir. Time to go."

Roberts jerked himself free. "Don't touch me. I'm leaving."

"Leave now," the guard warned, "Without another word, or I will use force." His finger stabbed in the direction of the door.

Robin stared at the closed door long after it shut behind them. Linda sat where Don had been and touched her hand. "I'm so sorry. All of his credentials checked out."

With a shaking hand, Robin brushed the hair off of her forehead. "I'm not doing something like this again."

Linda nodded. "I understand." She pressed some buttons on her phone. "Margaret? I need to talk to Mr. V. This isn't good."

Without waiting for Linda to hang up the phone or Tony to come gallantly into the room, Robin gathered her bag and her coat and left. Linda tried to call her back, but she was stuck on hold with Tony's office. Escape. Flee. Hide.

The elevator arrived. Thankful to find it empty, she slipped inside and pressed the lobby button, then the door close button in rapid succession. As soon as it started moving, she went to the back corner of the elevator and pressed back against the wall. She used to be good at hiding. Hide way in the back of the closet. Protect her sisters. Make the monsters forget you're there.

But she couldn't hide from her past, could she? What did she think she was doing, becoming Mrs. Antonio Viscolli? Inadequate didn't begin to describe her. Her cell phone started ringing, but she turned it off as she stepped off of the elevator and into the lobby of the hotel. As she walked out of the doors, the valet lifted his hand in greeting, grabbed her keys, and rushed to get her car. With no choice but to wait, she slipped her coat on and shoved her hands into the pockets, lifting her shoulders against the wind. Before her car arrived, she felt Tony at her elbow.

"I'm sorry."

"I'm not doing that again."

"It will never happen again."

Robin turned her head and looked him straight in the eye. "Oh, I know it won't."

Her car pulled up in front of them. Tony touched her elbow. "Robin, please."

"It's okay. I have to go now. But I'll see you when you get back from California." He looked so worried and a frown marred his forehead. Putting a hand on his cheek, loving him, needing him, she pressed her lips to his. "I love you. Have a safe trip."

CHAPTER SEVEN

Maxine stood back and declared, "That one."

Robin stood on the platform staring at multiple reflections of herself wearing dress number nineteen thousand three hundred and two. Or maybe just the fifth one. Perhaps it just felt like nineteen thousand or so after all the pictures and websites and magazines and now the trying on. Perhaps she was just remembering the approximate price tag. The five dresses combined probably cost more than she paid for Maxine's first four semesters.

Sarah walked around the platform, surveying the ivory dress, running her fingers over the intricate beadwork on the long train. "Oh yes," she breathed. "This one."

Robin looked in the mirror directly in front of her. The sleeveless bodice almost formed a heart shape and cinched tight at her waist. The skirt flared out, split in the front to show an underskirt of the same material. The edges were scalloped, and tiny pearly beads were sewn into patterns and swirls all over the skirt and train. She felt amazing and beautiful in this dress.

"I don't know if I like the sleeveless," she said, touching her shoulders.

"You'll like it when you see the pictures," Maxine said. "Are you going to wear the necklace from Tony?"

Robin snorted. "Which one?" Maxine raised an eyebrow. "Of course, silly. The Valentine necklace. How could I not?"

"The way the bodice makes the heart shape will seriously make that necklace look like it was made for this dress." Sarah lifted her own curls. "And up. You need your hair up."

Maxine nodded. "Absolutely. My hairdresser is already arranged. You're meeting her next week to discuss hairstyle."

Hairstyle? Robin almost groaned. "Isn't my hair going to be under a veil? What difference does it make how it's up or styled under a veil?"

"I'm going to pretend you didn't say that." Maxine hooked her arm over Sarah's shoulders. "Tony is going to flip."

Sarah nodded. "Kind of like he did with that red dress."

"Yeah. I don't mean to brag," Maxine bragged, "but that red dress was the best idea I've had in a long time."

"Amen, sister." Sarah pulled out her phone and checked an incoming text. "We have an appointment at the hotel tomorrow morning to look at flowers," she said as she replied to the text. "Don't forget."

Robin pulled her hair up and looked at the reflection from every angle. "How could I forget? I don't even remember what my office looks like anymore. All I know is this wedding."

"Poor, poor, Robin. Don't worry. In two months it will

be over and we can quit hearing you gripe about the hardship of it." Maxine waved the sales clerk over and her tone grew a bit less sarcastic and a bit more scolding. "You're planning a wedding so you can marry a hard working and Godly man who has the means to fly you to New York City in his private jet for a Valentine's Day dinner. Most women would kill or die for that. You need to lighten up and stop being such a wet blanket. Let us enjoy it, at least."

Robin felt contrite. She thought about what being wife to that man meant and her mind went back to the horrible interview. She put a hand to her forehead as a headache suddenly sprang up and assaulted the area behind her eyes. She heard Maxine speak to the store clerk. "We have a winner. It's going to need some minor alterations."

"Excellent," the tailor said. "I'll tell you in confidence, of the five you selected, this one was my very favorite. I'll just get my tape and some pins."

AS they walked into Cassandra's office in the administrative area of the Viscolli Hotel, Stephanie said, "I took your idea for red roses. I think you'll be pleased."

Cassandra met them at the door. "Ladies, if you'll follow me, please. I have a room with the same carpet and wall colors as the Grand Ballroom where I've set three different tables. You can choose the table settings and flowers, mix and match, whatever you want to do."

Robin quickly chose the ivory colored gold rimmed china for the place settings. She and Maxine and Sarah moved flowers around and finally settled on an arrangement of ivory roses in the shape of a ball that sat in a tall stand. Cream colored table clothes with gold accent covers would look very elegant in the grand ballroom.

The bridal table would have an arrangement of red and ivory roses that would run the entire length of the long table.

"Your bouquet," Stephanie said, "will be red and white roses, similar to the bridal table."

"Are we overdoing the red?" Robin asked.

"Oh no. The room is huge with vaulted ceilings. I think the red will just compliment the gold and cream nicely," Cassandra said.

Stephanie opened a leather portfolio and pulled out a card stock. "Here is the invitation sample. I have a calligrapher coming tomorrow to start working on addressing the envelopes."

Robin took the invitation. On heavy off-white colored paper lined with gold ribbon were the words:

Miss Robin Bartlett
and
Mister Antonio Viscolli
request the honor of your presence
as they come together before family and friends
in the sight of God
to be joined together in Holy matrimony
Saturday, April 21st
at four o'clock in the afternoon
Boston Central Bible Church
Boston, Massachusetts

Reception immediately to follow
at the Viscolli Hotel, Boston

*"So they are no longer two, but one.
Therefore, what God has joined together, let man not
separate."*
Matthew 19:6

"These are absolutely beautiful," Robin said, running a finger over the gold ribbon. "I can't believe how nicely they turned out."

"I agree. They are lovely. They'll go out the first of March," Stephanie said.

"How many names did Tony whittle his list down to?" Maxine asked.

Cassandra laughed. "Eight hundred. But—" she said, holding up a hand to forestall Robin's protest, "not everyone will RSVP."

"Maybe not, but we have an open invite going to the church, too," Robin said.

"Oh, right," Cassandra said. "I'd forgotten that part." She made a notation in her book. "Well, if we have to, we'll open the doors and set up the tents. But, I'm sure we'll be fine."

Stephanie gestured to another table. "Here are some favor options I've worked on with Cassandra." On a tray lay strawberries dipped in white and dark chocolate that had been decorated to look like wedding dresses and tuxedos, handmade chocolates, and some wedding themed cookies. "My personal favorite is the strawberries."

"What are favors?" Robin asked.

Sarah said, "They're gifts you give the guests. It's just something fun." She pointed to the tray. "Those strawberries are amazing."

Maxine looked over Sarah's shoulder. "They are. I'd go with the strawberries."

Robin worried she'd forget some other detail she didn't know anything about—like favors for guests. "Okay. We'll go with the strawberries."

A waiter wheeled in a service cart. Cassandra clapped her hands in glee. "Awesome. Thank you, Ben."

"My pleasure, Cassandra. Radio when you want me to clear." He left.

Cassandra put a gentle hand on Robin's forearm. "This is the tasting of the menu! These are some of my all time favorite sides."

Four covered dishes sat on the cart. Cassandra removed all of the covers. One plate held a sampling of hors d'œuvres and canapés from caviar topped crackers to smoked salmon bites. One plate held a small lamb chop sitting on a bed of chick peas next to roast quail with some spring greens. Asparagus draped over cauliflower mashed potatoes added more green to the plate. Another plate had the vegetarian sampler, with a falafel and some vegetarian labneh yogurt sauce, polenta on a bed of greens, and some asparagus. Maxine and Robin grabbed forks and napkins and tasted the meats, leaving Sarah to sample the vegetarian plate.

"This is amazing," Robin said before swallowing a tender bite of lamb seasoned perfectly with rosemary and garlic.

"I love that you went with lamb instead of beef," Stephanie said. "It will be something different."

Sarah dipped another bite of falafel into the labneh. "Oh wow," she said, mouth full. "I can't believe how good this is."

Cassandra grinned. "We have a chef from Dubai. The things that he can create starting with dried garbanzos would make you cry."

"This quail is so moist," Maxine said. "It's always dry whenever I've eaten it before."

"That will certainly be the challenge for the chef. Poultry can dry quickly. As you can see, though, that is moist and wonderful, and was plated about ten minutes ago. I think we'll be okay."

Robin nodded after taking the offered bite from Maxine. "I agree." She wiped her fingers on a cloth napkin. "What's under those domes?" she asked.

Cassandra used exaggerated motions to lift the silver lid. "Cake!" She said, dimples appearing on her round cheeks. "We have French Vanilla with a Chocolate Mousse, Red Velvet with Infused Whipped Cream, and Chocolate Fudge with Peanut Butter Mousse."

Robin took a small bite of the chocolate with the peanut butter and thought her tongue was going to just start dancing inside her head. "Oh my," she said. "This is wonderful. But someone might have a peanut allergy."

"The servers will all have careful instructions. Not to worry."

Maxine tasted the red velvet. "Oh! Oh, man. Oh my stars. Robin? You have got to taste this," she said, holding the fork out to Robin. She looked at Sarah. "No cake for you?"

Sarah held up her hand, palm out. "No. None."

Robin snapped her fingers as she swallowed the most heavenly bite of red velvet she'd ever tasted. "Oh, right. Eggs and milk." She looked at Cassandra. "We'll need a vegan tier."

"No we don't," Sarah said.

Robin winked. "Yes, we do. My sister is having cake at my wedding." She waved a hand over the samples. "I say yes to them all. The cake is going to have eight tiers. It's not like there's not room for different flavors."

Cassandra laughed and made a notation while Stephanie said, "If all of my clients were as easy as you."

DERRICK DiNunzio waited in the reception area just outside of Tony Viscolli's office on the top floor of the Viscolli Hotel, Boston. He wore a long coat with tails and held a top-hat in his gloved hands. For the last few days, he had been learning how to be a doorman and greeter for the hotel.

Over two months had gone by since Derrick had shown up right here in this office. Tony had offered him a salaried position with full benefits. He laid out a plan for Derrick's life for the next 3 years. Tony had hired a private education center to determine Derrick's strengths and weaknesses. Almost immediately, he started working with them.

"I've already worked with these people," Tony had said. "You know Sarah. She's going to be a nurse and these folks are optimizing her time and classes so she can get intern hours under her belt for credits, too. I think they are good choice for what we will do with you."

Derrick went to the private education center every day for two weeks and sat for test after test after test. With his results in hand, the specialists at the center set about getting Derrick on track to obtain his General Education Degree, the equivalent of a High School Diploma. He needed it since he had dropped out of school a few years earlier.

Once he had his GED, he would attend online and on-site classes five days a week in order to sit for tests called CLEP tests. Passing these tests meant he would earn equivalent college credits in fundamental areas like mathematics and English without having to attend the actual classes. At the end of this road, Derrick had a full blown college education and a college degree waiting for him. And once he had that sheepskin, Tony assured him that the sky was the limit.

When Derrick got back to the apartment one night, he tried to talk about it with the only person there, Sarah Thomas. After Robin and Tony married, Sarah would move in to the room down the hall from his. She had planted herself in Tony's apartment that afternoon after having met with her interior decorator. Sarah was a few years older than him but much shorter, and he felt like she was approachable like her sisters. They had gotten off on the wrong foot when they first met, but he knew he could correct that given time. Derrick started talking and she let him speak until he started feeling uncomfortable with her impenetrable silence and stoic expression.

When he finished, she had said, "Wow. You dropped out of high school? Color me surprised."

Derrick had stared at her, not fully believing the depth of her hostility. Then he had nodded and said, "Yeah. I figured I needed the extra time to work on my tattoos, sweetheart."

Derrick had taken Tony up on his offer. Perhaps ironically, he had taken to his new lifestyle as if born to middle class parents in the suburbs. Comparing himself to Tony Viscolli with his super sharp appearance, Derrick had made every effort to clean up his own personal grooming. Granted, some things took some getting used to for him.

Derrick no longer had to worry about where his next meal might come from. He hesitated for long minutes the first time he realized that he should just go ahead and dispose of the disposable razor that had shaved its last good shave. Now, a fresh razor and a hot shower were only ever a few minutes away. Fresh, clean, brand new clothes that fit him as if tailor made were his for the asking. And shoes—shoes that looked so very nice and felt so incredibly good on his feet—shoes that no foot but his own had ever worn before surrounded his feet in the company of thick, warm socks. For Derrick, these things alone amounted to luxuries of untold worth.

Tony's secretary answered a quick call in her headset then caught Derrick's eye. "He'll see you now, Mr. DiNunzio."

Mr. DiNunzio. Derrick had been called much, much worse in his lifetime. He felt unexpectedly nervous about seeing Tony in his office. He saw him every evening when Tony was in town, shared a meal with him if his shifts at the hotel allowed it. But they never talked business at home, always God or sports or something else.

He knew that he hadn't done anything wrong. Intellectually, he knew that Tony would not have Derrick "tuned up" as they said in his neighborhood, or worse. He could not identify the source of the butterflies in his stomach or the feeling of apprehension that kept him checking the corners of his eyesight.

He strode into the office and Tony rose with a smile and extended his hand. "Derrick, *figlio*. So good to see you. I must say that uniform seems to suit you. How is it going? Learning the ropes?"

Derrick took Tony's manicured hand in his own white gloved hand and they shook. "It's fine, sir. All the guests are nice, and often tip, and all the people manning the concierge station are helping me a lot."

Tony nodded. "Good. Good. I want you to do that for at least a few more weeks. Let me know when you are ready for a new challenge. I want you to work with the wait staff some more, too. Your speech lessons are really paying off. Your inflection is nearly perfect. Sit. Sit." He gestured toward the couch.

Derrick reached behind him and picked up his tails with one hand before taking a seat. "Is that what you wanted to see me about, Mr. Viscolli?"

Tony resumed his place behind his desk. "Not everything. There is some more. I wanted you to know that I heard from the ed center this morning. I wanted to be the first to congratulate you on earning your GED. It seems you were a good investment on my part. I'm very proud of you."

Derrick felt amazement and, as that feeling surfaced, a lot of his unexplained anxiety vanished. "Really? I thought we'd hear back next week."

Tony smiled, "They have your diploma ready. You can pick it up tonight when you go in for your first CLEP class."

"That's awesome, Mr. V. I don't know what to say. Thank you so much! Thank you. I never would have done anything like this without you."

Tony put his hand up in a calming gesture, "*Non ne parliamo.* Just keep working hard."

"I will, Mr. V. I promise."

Tony nodded, then he grew solemn and said, "Derrick, that isn't the only reason I asked you to see me this morning. I need to ask you something very serious, now. And I want you to know that your answer can be 'no' and nothing will change. I want you to trust me when I say that."

The anxiety Derrick felt suddenly returned full force. He had been waiting and waiting here in Never-never-land for the other shoe to drop. Billionaires didn't just give people anything. They loaned. And loans came due—with interest. A good investment? Yeah. If Derrick had learned anything in his life on the streets it was that the reason rich people stayed rich is because they didn't give anything away. Ever.

So this was when Tony would ask him to go do something that he, himself, could not be party to for risk of getting his squeaky-clean filthy-rich hands dirty. This was payback time. This was when Tony asked Derrick to beat someone up, or threaten someone, or courier some merchandise, or even kill someone. Derrick had dreaded this moment but he braced himself for what was to come. Because Derrick had no illusions about judging a book by its cover. One could never tell what the book said inside but one could always tell what the book was going to cost. He knew how much this deal could cost him when he accepted the terms weeks before. And Derrick had never, ever welshed on a deal.

His voice came out ragged and scratchy and he asked, "What is it, Tony?"

Tony grinned, "Tony, now, is it? That's fine but not in front of any of your coworkers. Only in private. I have a public image, after all."

"Sorry." Derrick quickly said. He imagined that Tony Viscolli did have quite a public image to maintain. He braced himself to play his part in maintaining that public image. No one would ever know what he did to repay this man's patronage.

Tony shook his head. "Don't be sorry, *figlio*. You and I are like brothers. It is right that my brother address me in that way. But not so when I am the boss. Regardless, this is my question. As my brother, I am requesting that you stand beside me on the most important day of my life. You would deeply honor me if you could act as one of my groomsmen. Please set aside anything else, and just consider it."

Of all the things in the world that Tony could have asked him to do, this was as far away from any possibility he could have predicted as the east is from the west. Derrick had no idea how long he sat there with a dumb look on his face before he blurted, "You can't know how much it means to me that you asked me, Tony. I can't believe it. Of course. Of course I will."

Tony felt one corner of his mouth creep up. "Ah, well, I think you might have agreed too soon. I had not yet informed you that you will have to walk down the aisle beside Sarah."

And so the other shoe finally dropped. Derrick nearly laughed.

CHAPTER EIGHT

Robin rubbed her hands together then gripped her coffee cup in both hands, trying to warm them. From the window of the little cafe, she could see the river. It looked exactly as cold outside as it felt. Chunks of ice still floated near the shore of the Charles River, but the trees had started budding as spring desperately tried to beat back winter.

Tony carried two fresh steaming cups of coffee to the table and took his seat across from her. "This is a neat place," Robin said, admiring the comfortable interior with hard wood floors, couches, leather chairs, and bookshelves lined with eclectic reading selections.

Tony nodded. "The church runs it. It's a nonprofit so all receipts and tips support overseas ministries. We have a lot of handmade art and jewelry that are made by girls in a pregnancy crisis center in Africa. Those are sold here, too."

Robin looked closer at the decor and noticed the price tags. "Wow. This is incredible."

"Coffee houses are in vogue. We're just leveraging that

popularity until it stops meeting with success. It's all about the right marketing at the right time to the right audience." He took a sip of his coffee. "Plus, they make excellent coffee and scones."

She took a sip of the coffee and nodded. "That is good."

"I come here after rowing. I keep my scull in the boat house next door."

"It won't be long until you can be out there."

"I think I have another trip to Florida and some more wind surfing to do while that ice out there keeps melting." He lifted his cup as if in a toast and she laughed.

She set her cup back down in front of her. "How did the meeting with Derrick go?"

"It went well. I have a feeling that he thought I was about to hand him a bill for services rendered and was about to ask him to do something terrible. As soon as he realized nothing has changed, he relaxed so much. I hope he trusts me one day."

"He comes from a world where you don't get something for nothing."

"It isn't for nothing. I expect him to work hard and aim for success."

Robin laughed. "Tony, you know what I meant."

He leaned back as the waitress brought their scones. Steam piped up from them and Robin's mouth watered at the smell of fresh baked yumminess. "Of course I know what you meant," he said, breaking the blueberry scone in half and moving half to his plate, then breaking the cranberry scone in half and moving half to her plate.

"You don't mind, do you, that I asked him to move into our apartment? I know we'll be newlyweds."

Robin shrugged as she took her first heavenly bite of

light, flaky, blueberry flavored scone. She washed it down with the amazing coffee and just let the flavors mingle on her tongue for a moment before answering. "I don't mind. I guess we could have gotten him some apartment somewhere and done the same for Sarah, but I don't feel right about doing that. I think we need to just live together, the four of us. Derrick needs the family structure, and I want to get to know Sarah better now that I'm not juggling two jobs and scraping a living."

Tony finished off the half of cranberry scone then set his fork down. "I want to talk to you about something."

"Okay." Robin set her own fork down and picked up her cup, sitting back in the chair.

"About the interview—"

With a sigh, Robin rubbed her temple with one hand. "You've managed to avoid talking to me about that. I was hoping it would go away."

"That's what I wanted to talk about." He placed his palm flat on the table in front of him. "People dig things up on me. It is inevitable. Who is this man slowly growing this fortune in this city with some of the biggest power players in the world? But, there was nothing to find out. I have no record, I have no paper trail. The best someone could do was to find my birth certificate, and that didn't tell them anything." He gestured at her with his palm. "You are a different story. You were in the system, so to speak. Your mother died as a tragic statistic. You were arrested after stabbing a foster father."

Robin snorted. "Yeah, and he—"

With a small smile, Tony said, "Yes. I know. The point is, people are going to dig, discover, and it's going to get out. The reporter was correct. I think you should be open about your past. Do another interview with him. We'll give it on the condition that we get to read the final product before publication. Stop the fire before it becomes a storm, so to speak."

Embarrassment, horror, fear, all sprang up in her chest, drowning her. "Wait. You can't be serious."

"I am completely serious." He reached for her hand and took it with both of his. "I can't stop this from happening. We can just try to control it."

Terrified that she would just burst into tears sitting right there, Robin closed her eyes and pulled her hand away. "Please," she whispered.

"My love, you have nothing for which you need be ashamed. You were a child and your story is a remarkable tale of endurance and sacrifice. You made it. Look at the woman you became."

He was right. They would never stop. The best defense was a good offense. She took deep long breaths. In and out. Inhale, exhale. Finally in control, she opened her eyes and looked at her fiancé. "If you think I need to, then I will. But I wish you didn't think I needed to."

"Robin, *cara*, I am sorry that it came to this, and I'm even sorrier that I didn't foresee it. Please forgive me."

This time, she reached forward and took his hand. "Tony, this isn't your fault. It's just life. And for whatever reason, people care about stuff like that. It's never been important to me, other peoples' stories. But I guess this is considered news. I trust your judgment in handling it, and I know you wouldn't put me in a position that would hurt me."

His eyes grew intense and Robin's heart skipped a beat. "Never," he said. "I promise you that."

"I just wish—"

Tony waited, but she didn't finish the sentence. Finally,

he asked, "What, *cara*? What do you wish?"

Robin picked her fork back up again and cut a piece of scone. "I just sometimes wish you weren't richer than dirt. Then I wouldn't have to worry about people questioning how genuine my love for you is or what my motivations might be for marrying you."

ROBIN leaned back against the booth as the waitress placed a salad in front of her. Craig sat across from her and fidgeted as the waitress gave him his soup. He picked up his spoon but set it back down again. "Can we bless this?"

"Absolutely," Robin said, lacing her fingers in her lap and bowing her head.

Craig cleared his throat and said, "Dear God, thank You for this food. And thank You for my daughter and for her birthday. I know my future is not bright, what with the prison sentence in front of me, but I'm glad to at least get this one with her. Amen."

Robin smiled and put a hand to her chest. "What a beautiful prayer. Thank you."

He shrugged, clearly uncomfortable. "This is all new to me. I don't always know what to say or how to act."

"Likewise."

With a nod, he picked up his spoon again. "That's right. It's new to you, too. You make it look easy."

"I have a good teacher," she said, looking at the ring on her finger. "Tony has been great."

"You got yerself a good man, there, girl. You keep him." He looked around the steak house. Loud country music blared from the speakers and peanut shells littered the floor. Robin loved the nostalgic post WWII decor and the relaxed atmosphere. "Pretty nice place, huh?"

"I think it's wonderful. Thank you for inviting me." She chewed on some iceberg lettuce and swallowed. "Can I ask you for a favor?"

"Sure." Craig took another sip of soup, then pushed his bowl aside.

"Well, two things, really." She was still trying to learn how to relate to her only living parent.

"Anything." His fingers tapped on the top of the table. Robin had noticed that he never sat still anymore. She remembered all the years serving him at Hank's and could always tell when he had reached his drink tolerance, because his fidgety body would slowly slow down.

"I have four months left on my lease and don't really want to break it. Maxine's apartment is ready for her to start moving into it. I know the halfway house is pushing you to get out."

Craig nodded. "Now that I have a job, they need to free up the bed. It's been hard to find something temporary, knowing what May will bring."

"Well, Maxine has offered to let Sarah and I stay with her, if you would be willing to take over my lease. I know it's two bedrooms, instead of one, but I can pay half of the rent if you need me to."

Craig nodded. "What's your rent there?" She told him. He frowned. "I might could swing it. I think Casey's being a little more generous with my pay because I'm the boss' dad." He grinned. "I'm okay with that, though, 'cause I won't be here for too long."

In a spontaneous movement, she reached forward and took his hand. "I'm really proud of you. You going forward to the police and turning yourself in is amazing."

With a shrug, he said, "I can't run anymore."

She squeezed his hand and went back to her salad.

"You're doing the right thing. But it must be intimidating."

"Well, I don't know. I been inside more of my adult life than out. So, it's not like an unknown. Would be better if I knew how long they's going to give me. Barry doesn't seem to think it will be more than ten years, seein's how I turned myself in and it's manslaughter. But, we'll see. What is going to be hard is to start a ministry inside. Abram and Tony, they're helping me and teaching me. I go to class every Wednesday to learn how."

Robin grinned. "I know. It's so exciting."

Craig shook his head and smiled at the same time. "So strange this turn in my life. But you know, we were praying about it and, this is going to sound funny."

Robin waited. When he didn't speak anymore, just kept his lips tight and his eyebrows knotted up, she prompted, "Go ahead."

He took a breath and raised one shoulder in a half shrug, "Well, it was like I heard someone talking to me inside my head. Like I heard an actual voice. It was telling me that I had already been to prison for a reason. That I already knew the system inside for a reason. That everything had already been planned ahead of time to bring me to this place and time that is coming. I can't get my head around it. I took two lives. It makes no sense to me. And since then, I find myself feeling excited about the idea of going back in. Imagine being excited about going back to prison."

"I know what you mean." Robin took a drink of her soda and pushed her plate aside just as the waitress arrived carrying platters of steak and potatoes. Her mouth watered at the tantalizing aromas wafting her way.

After she cut into her steak and chewed the first bite, she said, "I was also wondering if you wouldn't mind giving me away at my wedding. I'd contemplated asking Hank, but—"

He shook his head. "I ain't been much of a father to you. Hank did so much more."

"But you are my father. I'm incredibly proud of you and want to show you off. But also, I was praying about you or Hank and I kept hearing my voice saying I must honor you because you are my father." She watched as he tugged at his collar and nervously took a sip of his iced tea. "I spent so many years feeling like I was alone. In the last few months, I've gained Tony and his friends and now I've found my dad. I want you to be the one to give me away."

Craig's eyes blinked rapidly and he cleared his throat a few times before speaking. "I'd be honored," he whispered, then furiously cut into his steak.

TONY rose from the couch as Robin came into her apartment. "Hi. How did the dinner with Craig go?"

"Hi." Robin shed her coat and put her purse and keys on the bar dividing the kitchen and living room. "It was really nice. My steak was great."

"Is he going to give you away?" Robin walked toward him and put her arms around him, resting her head on his shoulder. She loved the way it felt when he put his arms around her, and for a moment, she just breathed in the smell and feel of him.

"Yes," she said, pulling back and kissing him. "He thought Hank should do it, but I convinced him. He's also going to take over my lease."

Tony frowned. "Your lease?"

Robin shrugged and waved her hand in a dismissive gesture. "Instead of breaking my lease at the end of April,

I'd rather give the apartment to Craig. Sarah and I are going to go stay with Maxine."

"Why didn't you come to me? I could have helped work this out. I could have gotten Craig a place, or you a hotel room or something."

"I don't know. Maybe because it doesn't have anything to do with you, and it was easy to work out?"

"*Cara*, everything pertaining to you pertains to me."

Robin sat down on the couch and raised an eyebrow. "Oh? Do you want to give me the specifics of your day and all of your wheeling and dealing, or do you plan to just gloss it over with your smooth voice and romantically tell me how the day stretched on and on in front of you until the moment you could see me again?"

Tony stared at her for a moment before throwing his head back and laughing. "*Touché*," he said. "Point made and point taken." He sat next to her and pulled a box out of his jacket pocket. "Happy Birthday, my beautiful bride-to-be."

Her knee-jerk was to complain about yet another expensive gift, but since it was her birthday, she grinned and took the box from him. Inside, nestled in tissue paper, was a business card. "What is this?"

"That is an all-inclusive spa weekend for you and your sisters to be taken at some point before the wedding. It includes—for each of you—a 90 minute full body massage, masks, hair and nail stuff—all that spa things that I am told women most enjoy. This place is supposed to be the spot to go to in Boston."

Robin read the business card. "So I just call the number."

"*Sì*. The reservation for the three of you is under your name."

She put her arms around his neck and said, "Thank

you, for my present."

"You are most welcome. I confess, I find that I am curious to see how much more relaxed you feel after enjoying your spa day with your sisters."

ROBIN sat in Stephanie Giordano's cute little office. All around her were pictures of weddings, parties, even elaborate birthday parties for children. Material lay draped over a couch in a corner and boxes of stuff from a company with the tag line "Your entertainment headquarters" were stacked in a corner.

Stephanie used a key to unlock a filing cabinet drawer, and pulled out four jewelry boxes. "I love that you used the necklace Tony gave you for Valentine's Day to design your bridesmaid gifts," she said. "My jeweler really enjoyed doing this."

"I'm so glad. The necklace is so pretty, and the dress I picked out just fits it so well that I wanted to keep the look flowing," Robin said, reaching for one of the boxes. She opened the top and smiled. An outline of a heart made out of alternating diamonds and rubies hung suspended from a silver chain. It was exactly the size and shape of the diamond heart on Robin's ruby and diamond necklace. "This is perfect!" she said.

"I think it will go nicely with the dresses you picked out for the girls, too," Stephanie said. "Here is the locket for the flower girl." Robin had also commissioned a silver locket for Angel Dove that contained a photo of Peter and Caroline. She opened the locket and smiled. "It's a little large for such a small girl, but I'm sure it will be something she treasures as she gets older."

"I love it," Robin said. "It was exactly what I had in

mind."

Stephanie opened a file folder. "Tony's office sent me the order of ceremonies. Here is a sample of the printed program." She handed Robin a heavy card stock folded in half the color of rich rubies.

In formal white scrolling letters on the front it read, "The Wedding of Robin Bartlett and Antonio Viscolli," listing the names and addresses of the church and the hotel. Inside on the left, it listed the wedding party, and on the right it gave an order of service, from the invocation through the solos and message, to the vows, more singing, and the presentation of the bride and groom.

"I love this paper," Robin said. "I'm surprised it doesn't feel like too much red."

"I think red ink on white paper would have felt like too much red. This feels very elegant." Stephanie handed her another sheet of paper. "These are the shots the photographer is going to want before the ceremony. We'll take all the photos of you with or without your party that will not have Tony in them before the ceremony, so we don't tie up the time before the reception taking pictures."

"This is all very real," Robin said. "I can't believe we're just a month out."

"Oh, speaking of, I wanted to let you know that we are definitely going to have to put out heated tents at the hotel. RSVP's are coming in and we're pushing close to the limit of the capacity for the room, and that doesn't include the open invite to the church."

Robin nodded. "I had a feeling Tony wouldn't be able to streamline his list enough." She settled back in the chair. "He likes hosting parties far too much."

Stephanie laughed. "You know, you have been a joy to work with on this. I was so worried it would be a bear and my business would be ruined."

"Well, I don't know what I'm doing. I've never even been to a wedding. So, it's easy to concede to your judgment, since this is what you do for a living." Robin made a note in her notebook. "I still need to get with Tony about our vows. And, on the checklist you gave me, it said something about toasts?"

"You and Tony need to decide who is going to give toasts, and make sure they know it. Traditionally, it's the best man. It can also be your father, your maid of honor, whomever. You just need to make sure that is all arranged ahead of time."

As Robin put the jewelry boxes in her purse and stood to go, Stephanie snapped her fingers. "One other thing. Are you free on the second of April at two?"

Robin checked her phone. "I can be free," she said. "The restaurant is closed Mondays."

"Okay, good. Can you meet here at two to talk to your hair stylist again and meet your makeup artist?"

With a shrug, Robin made the notation in her phone. "I can be here."

"I should have your veil then. We can show it to the hair stylist and let her work your hair around the veil."

Robin put a hand to her hair. "It seems silly to focus so much on hair that will be covered the whole time."

Stephanie laughed. "It does. But you won't be wearing your veil for some of the pictures, and you won't be wearing it at the reception."

"I guess. And Maxine said something about nails?"

"Yes. The makeup artist will talk with you about that in some detail." Stephanie made a notation in her pad. "I will be with you for the conversation with them, so they'll know exactly what you want."

Robin laughed. "You mean, you'll tell me exactly what I want."

"Only because you have given me permission to do so." She walked around her desk. "Thank you for giving me this opportunity."

Robin gladly took the older woman's hand. "Thank you for taking such good care of me."

She left the building and slid onto the electronically warmed leather seat of her luxury sedan. It occurred to her that it had been well over a month since her car broke down. She loved her sleek little sapphire blue sedan as much as Tony likely knew she'd love it, and couldn't stand the idea of going back to her rusty old trouble making car. With a sigh and a smile, she figured Tony likely knew that, too. She bet that if she asked him, her car had already been repaired and was sitting in some parking lot somewhere just waiting for word from him to bring it to her or take it away forever. In the space of a heartbeat, she decided she'd tell him just to take it away forever.

She drove home in her new, safe, reliable car enjoying the brightness of the afternoon sun. She hoped to take the bright day as a sign that spring would come early. Then the weather would be so nice for the wedding that it somehow wouldn't matter that a few hundred guests would find themselves seated in tents.

After she arrived home, she went into her bedroom and stashed the jewelry boxes in her underwear drawer next to the jewels Tony had given her. She shut the drawer and worried, like always, that someone in her less than ideal neighborhood would realize they were in there and steal them. She was looking forward to being able to utilize Tony's security as a way for her to store her jewelry.

CHAPTER NINE

Barry shifted the end of the trunk in his hand and said, "Wait a second. Okay. Go." At the other end of the trunk, Derrick grunted and the two men slowly maneuvered out of the apartment.

"What is in this thing?" Derrick panted.

Sarah frowned at him. "Just books. Be careful with the trunk. It was a gift."

"We're being careful, sweetheart." Derrick carefully eased the trunk through the doorway. "We're being careful."

"I'm not your sweetheart." Sarah rolled her eyes at his back and turned to Robin. "I hate leaving with this much chaos going on."

Robin dismissed her with the wave of a hand. "You have a big test coming up. Go and study. I'll see you tonight."

Sarah hugged her quickly. "Okay. How about I bring dinner with me?"

"Yes. Do. Oh, from that sushi place you love so

much," Robin encouraged, waving as Sarah left. She put her hands on the small of her back and stretched. As soon as she removed her hands, she felt Tony put his fingers on her hips and use his thumbs to knead the aching muscles in the small of her back. Robin turned her head and smiled. "I'll give you about an hour to quit doing that," she said.

He smiled and pulled her back against him to kiss the back of her neck. "You should have let me hire movers."

"Too chaotic. Something would get messed up. Maxine going one way, Sarah and me going to Maxi's then to your apartment. Craig moving in. Easier if we just do it." She unbuttoned her blue flannel shirt and slipped it off her shoulders, leaving her wearing a gray T-shirt with her jeans. "But, my back does hurt. That ninety minute massage is looking really good right now."

Craig came in, carrying two big boxes. With a heave, he set them on the floor by the couch.

"Craig, do you want me to leave any furniture?" Robin asked.

"Sure. Whatever you don't want to move."

"Tony's place is fully furnished, and Maxine has been buying new things for her apartment, so I think if you want it, it can stay."

"Sure, yeah. Then, you know, whatever."

Robin grinned. "All-righty."

Tony put a hand on the back of her neck and squeezed. "I'm heading to the apartment. Do you want me to hand-carry anything that is going there instead of Maxine's?"

Robin snapped her fingers then took him by the hand. "Actually, yes. Come on back and I'll get them for you."

"What?"

She led Tony down the hall to her room, furnished

with a single bed on a metal frame and a worn-out dresser she bought at a thrift store. She opened the top drawer of her dresser and reached in but felt nothing. "Wait," she said.

"What?" Tony looked over her shoulder.

Frantic, Robin shifted underwear and socks around, but still felt nothing. "My necklaces," she said. "The ones you gave me, the gifts for the wedding party, your wedding ring, my passport—" Taking a deep breath and fighting back tears, she started pulling one piece of clothing out at a time. "I put them all here."

"Maybe you moved them." Tony started helping her, looking through the piles of clothes.

"No. I've been putting them here since you've been giving me gifts. I don't have anywhere else to put them."

"Maybe someone else removed them?"

Robin stepped back and put her hands on her hips. "No one knew they were there." She put her hands on the sides of her head. "Tony..."

"It's okay, *cara*. No reason to panic. We have a full three weeks before the wedding. That's plenty of time to replace anything." He put his hands on her shoulders and squeezed.

"That doesn't change the fact that they were here and now they're gone."

Barry popped his head around the corner of the door. He started to speak but looked at Robin's face. "Something wrong?"

"All my jewelry is missing."

Barry looked behind him and stepped into the room, shutting the door to a crack behind him. His presence seemed to occupy a third of the room. "Where was it?"

"In this drawer," Robin said, looking into it again as if

the jewelry would somehow magically appear. "Always in this drawer."

"Could someone else have packed it up?"

"No one knew it was here."

"Okay. It's just things," Tony said. "Unimportant in the long run."

"Things worth several thousand dollars, I imagine," Barry said. "Diamonds, sapphires, rubies… things that would be tempting for someone to take."

Robin narrowed her eyes. "What are you saying?"

"I'm saying that there have been a couple of people in and out of here that we don't know for certain we can trust just yet." Barry crossed his arms over his massive chest.

"A couple of people?" Tony asked.

Barry shrugged. "Sure. Craig, Derrick—I like them both and if they're sincere, they'll really do great things. But, what if they're not so sincere? What if the temptation of such a huge payday was too much to resist?"

Tony shook his head. "I trust Derrick implicitly—that is to say, as much as I trust you, Barry." He cocked his head. "And you and I both know how much I value and trust you."

Robin nodded. "I agree. There's no way Derrick would do that. I also think that if Craig—if my dad—were to take something like that, he wouldn't have stuck around for the theft to be discovered. He'd already be gone. So, I trust it wasn't him." Her phone vibrated in her pocket. She pulled it out and saw Sarah's face on the screen. "Hey, Sarah." she said as she answered it.

"Hey. I'm so sorry. I feel so stupid. I forgot to tell you that I packed your jewelry and passport up in my leather chest and locked it. The key is taped under the ice tray in the freezer. I just knew that boy Derrick was all over the apartment this morning and I just didn't trust him not to take them."

Robin felt her jaw clench. "I wish you would have told me before now," she said. "I have been in a panic looking for them."

"I'm so sorry. This test is really messing with my brain. There's my train. I love you. See you soon!" Sarah disconnected the call.

Robin put the phone back in her pocket. "Sarah packed them in that trunk you guys just took down," she said. "I knew no one would have taken them. At least, none of us would have."

"So did I," Tony agreed.

Barry gave a brief nod of his head. "I'm glad. Glad you found them."

ROBIN tossed her chopsticks into the empty carton of noodles and leaned back against the cushion on the floor. Sarah looked at another vegetarian California roll and Robin watched her debate before she finally picked it up and ate it. Maxine took a sip of her water and leaned against the wall.

"This apartment is fantastic," Sarah said.

"It was a steal of a find," Maxine agreed. "I am so excited about furnishing it and painting it. That wall over there," she said, pointing to the main interior wall of the living room, "is going to be red brick. I have a friend, well, a guy I dated once. He's a demolition guy for a construction company. I called him and he has a pile of bricks I can buy off of him from an old building on this street."

Robin said, "What about the other apartment, the one that you put the air mattress in for me?"

"I'm going to knock out some walls that join the two apartments, then make that one into an art studio." Maxine stood and started collecting empty boxes and cartons.

"This is like a dream for you, Maxi," Sarah said. "Everything about it, from Newbury Street, to your plans for a brick wall, everything is just so totally you."

Maxine grinned. "I know, right?"

She left the room with the empty containers and returned empty handed. Sarah stood and walked to a window, looking out at the pedestrian traffic. "Just think about how different things are now than just a year ago." She wrapped her arms around herself and turned to face her sisters. "I just want to say out loud, how much I needed you in my life, even when I didn't know it. I didn't know how to take it, that day you showed up. I didn't know how to relate to you when I started living with you. But the longer I am around you, the more I love and admire both of you." She gestured with her hand. "Maxi, I absolutely cannot wait to see what you do with this place."

"Thank you." Maxine went to her and hugged her tight. "I love you, too. You completed our family. I missed you so much when we were apart."

Robin pushed herself to her feet and joined her sisters at the window. "You two have been my life for so long that I don't know how to shift that focus to a husband."

Sarah reached out and tucked a strand of Robin's hair behind her ear. "The first thing you need to do is to quit resisting it. God brought you and Tony together with a very obvious purpose. Let Him work. Quit worrying about the little things."

"Like reporters who ambush me with questions they

shouldn't ask?" Robin felt her breath hitch with the memory.

"It doesn't matter. Just cling to Tony, and you two will weather anything." Maxine slipped an arm around Robin's waist and Sarah's waist.

IF Don Roberts felt contrite in any way, his contrition did not manifest in his outward appearance. He looked calm and collected as he waited in the reception area in front of Margaret's desk, eager for a second chance to interview the future Mrs. Viscolli. He didn't greet Robin as she walked through and entered Tony's office, seemingly entirely focused on his legal pad and his phone. Robin found it a bit amusing that Margaret occasionally eyed him as if he were an unruly child whose parents had momentarily stepped away leaving him to create mischief.

Robin tapped on the door and entered in the same heartbeat and immediately felt more at ease when not only Tony greeted her, but Barry Anderson as well. Barry nodded his blond head and greeted her with a warm smile and a simple, "Robin."

She had no idea if she would make it through the next hour, but she had endured coaching and prompting for three hours yesterday at the hands of Linda Cross. Linda had instructed her in a process by which if Robin detected any emotional response to a question, she had to first silently deal with her emotions then, secondly, restate or rephrase the question for the sake of clarity. Only when she fully understood the question being asked was she to take the most important step. The most important thing she had to do was silently ask herself, "Do you feel comfortable answering this question?" Only if she felt comfortable answering did she even need to do so because if she wasn't comfortable answering a question, she could very easily refuse.

Robin had also learned the very valuable meaning behind the interrogative phrase, "Is this off the record?" They had practiced scenarios and Linda had coached her in many practical ways. To be fair, Robin felt considerably more prepared for this interview. However, none of that set her nervousness aside.

Tony took her hands in his own and guided Robin to his very own chair behind his very own desk. Robin took her seat and nervously fiddled with her ring as she placed her hands in her lap, until she remembered that she was simply playing a part and folded her hands neatly in her lap. She adjusted her posture, squaring her shoulders and breathing deep to relax her diaphragm. Tony gave her a confident wink. "Are you ready my darling?"

"I'm still very nervous." Robin confessed.

Tony shook his head, "You'll do fine. I know it."

The phone buzzed and Margaret announced, "Linda is on 3, sir."

Tony answered, "We're ready. Put her on speaker." There was a click and Tony asked, "Linda?"

Linda answered, "I'm ready."

Tony smiled, "All right. Let's pray." He gently retrieved Robin's hand before he closed his eyes and bowed his head. As he began to pray, Robin followed suit. "God in heaven, we petition You that all of our speech and actions during this interview glorify and bring honor to Your holy name. We pray in one voice that You remove any fear, any doubt, any anxiety and we also pray for Don Roberts that he will see and hear only Your mighty voice. Father, we have petitioned You and we are faithful that You hear this prayer and that You will use us to work for Your kingdom in a glorious and miraculous way because we love You so and we ask these things in Your holy name, in the name of the Holy Spirit, and in the name of Jesus Christ. Amen."

With his concluding word, Robin suddenly realized that all of her butterflies were gone. She opened her eyes and realized that Barry had moved to take Tony's other hand. She had not heard him even move which, for a man of his size, could be disconcerting. They released hands and her fingers didn't tremble. Robin literally could not have been more ready for this interview and she said as much. "I didn't realize you were going to pray, Tony. I should have realized it. I'm ready, now."

Tony announced to the speakerphone, "Linda? Go ahead and bring Don in when you come up."

Before she disconnected, Linda acknowledged, "Yes, sir, Mr. V."

The office door opened and Robin calmly observed Don Roberts precede Linda Cross as they entered the space. Her thick square glasses turned toward Robin and she gestured Don to the chair in front of the desk but Barry intercepted him.

"Mr. Roberts. My name is Barry Anderson. I am the corporate attorney for Viscolli Enterprises." Don Roberts naively took Barry's offered handshake, a tactical error the journalist would regret over the course of the next several minutes.

Barry kept his voice even and emotionless as he gripped the man's hand. "As you know, I've already spoken with your editor and he assured me that he has already spoken with you as well."

The color began to drain from Don Robert's face when

he suddenly realized that he had inserted his right hand into an inescapable vice. Barry didn't even increase his grip because that would have likely broken bones, but his grasp left no doubt as to who was in charge of the conversation.

"Miss Bartlett is prepared to answer every civil question you have for her today... provided they are questions..." When Barry paused for effect, Don's knuckles turned bright red, his fingertips turned a funny shade of purple, and his fingers themselves turned chalk white. "... and civil."

Don Roberts nodded his head energetically, clearly wishing he had not taken the giant's hand in the first place.

Barry cocked his head and asked, "Must I elaborate, Mr. Roberts, or have you a sufficient understanding of what will occur should this interview take an unexpected turn?"

Clearly trying not to let his discomfort seep into his voice, Don assured, "I'm good."

Barry grinned and released the smaller man's hand, admiring the newshound's mettle despite himself. "Then we should probably get started."

Linda walked around the desk and flanked Robin's left. Standing to her right, Tony casually placed a hand on the back of her chair. Barry waited until Don had seated himself before likewise taking his seat.

As Don set his phone out, he said, "Miss Bartlett, we obviously got off on the wrong foot last time. I want to apologize for that. I also want to thank you for asking me back today. I want you to know that I really do have your best interest at heart. I am not an unethical man."

After a few heartbeats, Robin licked her lips and said, "Okay."

Don fiddled with his phone and set it down then

consulted his legal pad. Robin assumed that he had once more set his phone to record the interview. "So do you go by Robin or does Tony have a nickname for you, Miss Bartlett?"

Robin said, "Tony calls me *cara*. But Robin is fine."

Don jotted something then asked, "Robin, our readers will certainly want to know how the two of you met."

Robin spent a minute processing the essay question. "The first time we were formally introduced I was waiting on his table at a Chamber of Commerce breakfast that he sponsored. We had actually met the night before when he came to Hank's Place where I tended bar at the time."

"And that was last fall?" Don prompted.

"Yes, last fall."

"Then, he proposed on Christmas Eve while the two of you were vacationing in the Florida Keys?"

Robin said, "No."

Don looked up from his legal pad, "No?"

"The two of us weren't vacationing. Tony sponsors a trip to the Florida Keys for several foster children every year. This past Christmas season, he invited my sisters and me to join him on that trip. Since all of us came from a similar background as those kids, we took him up on his generous offer."

Don scribbled out something and said, "Oh, I see. So it wasn't just the two of you."

Barry shifted in his chair, crossing one giant leg over the other. Tony's face remained impassive. Robin didn't say another word.

"That's really nice," Don smiled. "Could you tell me more about the foster children?"

Robin processed the question and realized that the Holy Spirit was guiding her answers, "One of the things I admire about Tony is his heart for children. He supports hundreds of homes like the one here at Boston Bible that give children like my sisters and I once were a clean, safe, loving environment. I can't wait to support him in those ministries as his wife."

"Do you think the fact that you and Tony share such similar childhood experiences helped draw the two of you together?"

Robin tilted her head slightly and considered the question, "Are you asking if the fact that Tony and I both came from poverty is part of the attraction we feel for each other?"

Don nodded, his pencil poised. Robin said, "It certainly doesn't hurt."

Don asked, "So, if that's part of it, what's the rest? What do you think is his most attractive quality?" If he felt any discomfiture at posing the question with Tony Viscolli standing to her immediate right hand side, he showed none of it in his tone or expression.

Robin took a deep breath and decided to tell the truth. "Believe it or not, I didn't think I really found him that attractive at first. In hindsight, I realize that what I found most attractive—and still do to this very day—is his faith."

"His faith in you?"

Robin nearly laughed, "Certainly not, Mr. Roberts. His faith in God, specifically Yahweh, Jehovah, the creator of all things seen and unseen. His abiding and unshakable faith and his faithfulness to God is certainly the most attractive thing about my fiancée. Now that we share that faith, our lives can only get better."

Don sat back and lifted his pencil. "Well, I can't tell our readers that."

Robin considered that reply, then said, "I see.

Naturally, that is entirely up to you, Mr. Roberts. Of course, it is my answer—and it also happens to be entirely true."

Don considered that and said, "So are you guys Catholic or Protestant or what?"

Robin smiled and said, "If forced to answer I would have to say we are 'or what' since those kind of labels largely mean divisions and divisions usually mean disunity in the body of Christ. We're Christians."

The reporter consulted his notes, clearly having gone into an area he didn't want to explore further. "So you guys have set the date for April. Where are you registered?"

Robin smiled, "I can put you in touch with our wedding coordinator for all of your questions about those kinds of details. She's the best and I really can't imagine we'd be ready by April without all her hard work."

Don didn't even jot a note down. "Robin, our readers are going to want to know about your father. Anything you want to tell me about that?"

Robin pursed her lips. "Just that I'm proud of him."

Don sat up a bit straighter, "You're proud of him?"

Robin said, "Absolutely."

"Robin, your father was in prison for most of your childhood and has since confessed to the slaying of your mother and another man when you were fifteen. Can you tell me what you're proud of?"

Robin said, "Sure. The Craig Bartlett of my childhood was a thug. He was an addict and a very, very violent man. I never even really knew him as a child because when he wasn't in jail he was never a part of our lives. If he were still a violent addict, there would be almost nothing about him I could find honorable. The Craig Bartlett of today, the man I know, is not the man in the tabloid stories. My father turned himself in and confessed to all of his crimes without even trying to strike a deal. He is doing what he can to make restitution for his past wrongs. The way he has turned his life around despite his past, I have to say I'm proud of him. And I pray for him every day."

"Your parents were both addicts, Robin. Have you ever used drugs?"

Without hesitation, Robin answered, "Thankfully, I have not. I think the fact that most of the adults in my childhood succumbed to addiction is one of the big reasons I never wanted to experiment."

"But you were a bartender. Alcoholism is a much larger social problem than drug addiction in this country."

"You know, after Tony bought Hank's Place where I tended bar, one of the changes he made that really made me angry was he demolished the bar." Robin admitted. "At the time I didn't understand. All I saw was the loss of potential income from the higher tips a bartender can get. Now I understand, and I am so happy to have learned. I'm proud to manage Hank's Place without the bar."

"Have you decided who's going to take over at Hank's Place after the wedding?"

The question surprised Robin. "I'll still run Hank's. Why wouldn't I?"

The journalist looked skeptical. "So, you're like those lottery winners that swear up and down they won't quit their jobs?"

Robin grinned, "I don't play the lottery, Mr. Roberts. But I love Hank's Place. I can't imagine any good reason to ever quit."

"Robin, what can you tell our readers about stabbing your foster father in the back?"

Barry sat forward, "Don't answer that, Robin."

Robin said, "It's okay…"

Barry held up a massive hand, "No, it isn't okay. Mr. Roberts, if you want to discuss this topic, you had better go off the record. Otherwise, you may have to explain to a Superior Court Judge how you apparently committed or were complicitous in felonious access to sealed juvenile records."

Roberts glanced back at Robin and asked, "Off the record okay?"

Robin nodded, "It's fine."

Barry sat back but his eyes never left Roberts. Robin explained, "At the age of 15, there was a set of very specific circumstances that led to that act of self-defense. I really don't care to elaborate on the details of those circumstances, but I can tell you that if I had it to do over again with the same outcome, I would do it again."

"Why run from the law? If stabbing a person in the back could possibly be self defense, why not press charges?"

"Because I was a child, Mr. Roberts. A little girl. The only thing anyone had ever taught me about conflict by age 15 was to fight, hide, or run. And one thing I learned about fighting is never to get into a fight I might lose. So I ran and I hid."

Don retrieved his legal pad and pencil. "Can we go on record about how your former employer pulled strings with city hall to get you custody of your sister Maxine?"

Barry kept his tone droll, "You mean about her then minor child sister Maxine? That one?"

Don looked at Barry, his eyes not giving anything away, "It isn't like that."

Robin interjected, "Off the record, Mr. Roberts. I wanted custody of Maxine to get her out of those circumstances." Robin felt her eyes begin to tear up and she took a slow deep breath. "Off the record, Mr. Roberts. You wouldn't want anyone to live in those circumstances. The thing is, the vast majority of foster parents and adoptive parents are loving, giving, and caring people. They are skilled and they are, well, parents for lack of a better word. My youngest sister, Sarah, was adopted by a wonderful, caring, loving couple who couldn't have children of their own.

"But, Mr. Roberts, for all the good people in the system, there is a minority of foster parents who are not all of those things. Not at all. The fact is that my sister Maxine and I just happened to fall into one of those rare bad situations."

Robin felt Tony's hand on her shoulder, his fingers gently squeezing, reassuring. "Maybe it had something to do with the fact that the police recovered my sisters and me from a very bad neighborhood. We were in the back of a dark, moldy closet in a condemned shack strewn with cigarettes and drugs and booze—oh, and two dead bodies. Maybe that's why. Maybe not. Who can say? The fact is, we ended up going from an unbelievably horrible situation to one that was merely intolerable. And Mr. Roberts, I don't regret doing what I had to do to get myself and my sister out. And I owe Hank so much for his help. For the record, the greatest thing I've done in my life so far was getting custody of my sister, Maxine."

The journalist took his pencil and very obviously lined out through three lines of his notes. He poised his finger above his phone and asked, "For the record, Robin, when did you know your life was going to change?"

Robin sat back and nodded. Don hit the button on his phone to start recording again. Tony subtly removed his hand and Robin somehow knew that he had rested it back atop the chair, just inches away, ready to intervene and reassure her once more if she needed his touch. "Well, Mr. Roberts, the first inkling I had that my life was about to change forever was on Tony's birthday. My sister, Maxine, had invited him to stay and celebrate and she even baked him a cake."

CHAPTER TEN

Robin drove to the church, but it was entirely under protest. Maxine and Sarah had shown up at Hank's at five and insisted that she eat dinner with them. All she longed to do was go home and hide, to mull over that morning's interview until she dissected all of the things she probably said the wrong way. But, she couldn't go home, could she? She didn't even have a home anymore. She had an air mattress in what would be Maxine's art studio.

Sarah slid out of the back seat of the car and looked at her watch. "What time does your church start?"

Maxine got out of the passenger's seat. "Seven on Wednesdays."

"It's five after."

Robin laid her head on the steering wheel. "I have a headache. Why don't you two go on. I'll come back and get you."

"No you don't," Maxine said, opening the door. "There's headache pills in the glove box. Let's go in. You'll be glad you did."

Robin covered her eyes with the palms of her hands. "I don't think so."

"For days now you've been completely down," Maxine said. "Let's go inside. You'll feel a lot better when you do."

Sarah wrapped her scarf tighter around her neck. "Come on, Robin, it's cold out here."

Robin glared at Maxine. "No. I'm going home and going to bed. I'll be back to get you."

Maxine leaned forward and put her forehead on Robin's. "You have a church full of girlfriends throwing you a surprise bridal shower. You need to swallow some aspirin, slap on a smile, and come in like you've never been so surprised in your life."

Tears burned in Robin's throat. "I don't want to have a wedding shower," she said in a near whisper. "Why would you do this to me?"

"Because, sister, this is what brides let their Maids of Honor do. They get showers thrown in their honor, and they enjoy them." Maxine knelt at Robin's open door. "What is wrong with you? Don't you want to marry Tony?"

"Of course I do," Robin whispered. A tear slid down her cheek. "I just don't know if I can be Mrs. Tony Viscolli. Does that make sense?"

Maxine took her gloved hand. "I doubt Tony would have thought he could be Mr. Tony Viscolli, Captain of Industry, as few as just ten years ago. But, he is. Look at how well he handles it. You can do this. You're so smart, and so charming. And those people in there," she said, pointing to the church, "love you. Let them shower you with gifts that show you that love."

Robin scrubbed at her cheek and pushed herself out of the car. "Okay. I'm sorry I'm not as excited about all this as you think I should be. It's so much, and so daunting."

"But you're not alone," Sarah said, slipping an arm around her waist.

"No, you're not alone." Maxine put her arm around her waist on the other side of her, and the two of them hugged Robin close. She felt safe and secure in that moment.

They walked toward the building, arms entwined just like that, until they reached the door. Maxine opened it and let Robin precede her into the room. After a brief pause, forty women yelled, "Surprise!"

Robin laughed and acted properly surprised. She greeted and hugged her friends and acquaintances, working her way around the room. She finally sat next to her friend Sofia Rabinovich. "How are you doing, Robin?" Sofia asked.

"I'm exhausted and on the border of intimidated by the concept of my future," she said with a smile. "But this party has set everything to right again."

Sofia had brown hair lightly streaked with gray, a beautiful long face, and bright green eyes. Her husband, Abram, on staff at the church had mentored Tony in Old Testament studies and would be presiding over the marriage ceremony for them. "If you need someone to talk to, I'm here," Sofia said. "You know that Abram and I have been married for many years. I can talk or listen, whatever you need."

Robin took her hand and laid her head on her friend's shoulder. "Thank you," she said. "I don't know what I would do without you guys in my life."

Sofia patted her hand. "Likewise, my beautiful young friend."

The time came when the last hors d'ouvrés had been served and everyone was in a joyful mood. Jacqueline

Anderson had arrived perhaps 20 minutes late hauling three pink shirt boxes wrapped with cheetah print ribbons and bows. Jacqueline had once more introduced herself to Maxine, apparently not having remembered they had met at the potluck in this very same gymnasium a little over a month before. Jacqueline then attempted to sequester Robin and monopolize her time.

"Why roses?" Jacqueline asked. "It's not like you're on some strict budget or something. Who is your wedding planner? Seriously?"

At Maxine's less than subtle urgings, Sarah interrupted and engaged Jacqueline in one of the games. As soon as the game ended, Jacqueline marched straight back up to Robin to continue the interrogation.

"I know you'll honeymoon in Italy, but where do you think you'll vacation? Aspen? Rio? The South of France?"

"Florida," Robin answered.

Jacqueline let her look of disgust turn to one of just appalled. "Florida? What, exactly, is good about Florida? It's all New York snow birds and tourists."

"Tony proposed to me in Florida."

Jacqueline shook her head. "Thank goodness you have such a big heart to accept that kind of treatment. I would have insisted on proposing to me somewhere nice, at least. Listen, darling, when Better Homes does the photo shoot of the apartment next June, have you given any thought to the appointments and accessories? I only ask because you really want the space to reflect your more feminine tastes instead of Tony's more masculine decor. Trust me, they have enough of that from all the shoots of his office. Who's your decorator? Don't tell me you don't already have a decorator."

"We're using Tony's decorator." Robin answered sounding a bit puzzled.

"Betty?" Jacqueline quizzed. "You're using Betty Lamordio? She's a dinosaur. I can recommend someone if you like."

"What photo shoot in June?" Robin asked.

"Oh, Barry told me all about it. He had to handle all the releases. Something about a human interest piece on the lifestyles of the rich and famous. Anyway—"

Maxine interrupted and asked Jacqueline if she couldn't be a dear and help her set up for the next party game. Jacqueline smiled a smile that never touched her eyes and oh-so-graciously agreed. The game was hosted by Caroline O'Farrell who asked Robin a series of questions about her betrothed. Whenever she got a question wrong, Robin had to stuff a grape into her cheek but not eat it. Whenever she got one right, she could make anyone else in the room hold a grape in her mouth. The winner was determined when either all the questions had been asked or someone couldn't fit another grape inside her mouth.

The softballs came out early. "On what day month and year was Tony born? What kind of car does Tony drive? What is his favorite sport? What is his favorite meal?"

By the end of the softballs, Jacqueline was holding six grapes in her mouth and her eyes smoldered. Then the questions got harder. "Okay, Robin, what was the name of Tony's very first company?"

Robin didn't know the answer. She stuffed a grape into her mouth.

"What part of Italy did Tony's mother originally come from?"

Grape.

"How many companies does Tony presently own and

operate?"

Robin spoke around cheeks stuffed with grapes. "Fifty-six."

"Oh, no, honey. He owns 71 firms."

"What?"

"Yes, yes. Unless he bought something new or sold something since yesterday. Okay, got the grape in there? Okay, next is what is the symbol for Viscolli Enterprises on the New York Stock Exchange?"

After fourteen questions, Robin realized two things. She could fit no more than 11 grapes inside her mouth and she knew far less about the man she was going to marry in a few short weeks than she previously assumed. As soon as the game ended, and Robin and Jacqueline spit out their grapes, Jacqueline picked up exactly where they had left off with a kind of obsessiveness that infuriated Maxine.

"You simply must tell me some way I can be in your wedding party. What with my husband acting as the Best Man, it's only proper that I at least be a bride's maid. Although you really should consider how nice it would look to have you and Tony center stage reciting your vows flanked by my husband as his Best Man and me as your Matron of Honor. The brand new couple flanked by the old married couple. Can you imagine how nice that would look in the press releases?"

"Maxine is my maid of honor." Robin said.

"Who is Maxine?" Jacqueline asked in a distracted way.

At that point, Maxine handed Sarah a pad and pen with probably a little more force than she meant to use and walked between the two women. "I'm so sorry. I have to borrow my sister."

She escorted Robin back to the middle of the group which formed a rough circle and spoke over the dozens of conversations in the room. "All right everyone, it's time to open presents."

Robin tried to put Jacqueline Anderson out of her mind and focus on the fun of opening presents. Sarah sat next to her and wrote down who gave her what, and she unwrapped and unbagged item after item of fun presents: a heart-shaped photo frame, a wedding memories book, an awful clock that she just didn't know what to do with.

Maxine handed her a large flat pink box with a cheetah print ribbon, and she laughed at something Caroline O'Farrell said as she opened it. She brushed aside the tissue paper, and her face immediately fused with heat when she saw the white silk and lace. She quickly closed the top.

"What was that?" Sarah asked, pen ready.

"I don't—"

Maxine took it from her and opened the lid. A murmur of excitement and appreciation went through the ladies who saw her hold up a spaghetti strap on a pinafore before quickly putting it back in the box.

"I guessed on sizes," Jacqueline said from her vantage point behind Maxine. She did not sit in the circle with the other ladies. "I'm confident I guessed properly."

Maxine nodded. "I'm sure you did. You seem to be able to size people up rather well." She stacked the opened box on top of the two unopened and set them over with the already opened gifts table.

Robin cleared her throat. "What's next?" she asked, forcing a smile. Maxine met her eyes, conveying understanding and knowing, as she handed her a bag containing personalized stationary with the letter "V" and asked for another present, trying to put out of her mind the negligee sets and everything that they implied.

IN the nightmare, Robin fingered the satin spaghetti strap of the white silk gown she wore. Her finger ran over the frilly lace that barely covered the rise of her breasts. The stale smell of cigarette smoke and spilled cheap alcohol burned her nose. Confused, she looked around. Gin bottles, discarded needle, rubber hosing, an overflowing ashtray, a blackened spoon, and a yellow disposable lighter lay on top of the burned and scarred coffee table. A big rip on the brown plaid couch allowed stuffing to come out of the cushion.

Panicked, she started toward the kitchen, needing to get a garbage bag to clean up the mess before one of the little kids got to it. What if Maxine or Sarah pricked their skin on the needle? No telling how sick it could make them.

"Where you going, little girl?"

At the sound of that voice, she froze. Her heart stopped beating and her hands went ice cold. She wanted to run, she wanted to hide, but before she could force her feet to move, a strong calloused hand seized her upper arm with nicotine stained fingers in a mean, bruising grip. "I said where ya goin' little girl?"

He spun her around and red-rimmed yellow eyes looked her up and down, from her bare shoulders, down the skimpy white silk that brushed the top of her knees, to her bare feet. "Not so little though, are ya?"

His broken teeth were brown and yellow. A blistered tongue, burned from too many tries on an empty glass pipe, shot out to lick cracked lips. His foul breath reeked of cheap cigarettes and cheaper beer. Bitter bile rose up in the back of her throat and she tried to turn her head to get away from the smell.

"No, you're a woman. Or you will be, soon as I'm done with you." A hand gripped her breast, squeezed and twisted it until the pain made her vision gray. She realized that her nightgown had vanished. She screamed, but the sound was muffled by his hand.

Vomit clawed at her throat. She couldn't find her knife, the knife she had palmed in the garage that time. No matter how she resisted, she wasn't strong enough. She was never strong enough. A single tear rolled out of the corner of her eye while his gloating laughter echoed in her ears.

Suddenly, the ramshackle apartment vanished, replaced by the banks of the Charles River in the summertime. The warm sun shone down from a bright blue sky, and the softly blowing breeze caught the hem of her dress, slowly moving it around her bare legs.

Then his eyes changed. They turned from light blue, glassy, red-rimmed to chocolate dark. The putrid odor of his breath changed to faint peppermint. In the kind of transition that only makes sense in a dream, he wore white trousers and a white top, making his skin seem darker, his teeth whiter. Abruptly, his laughter no longer fell on her ears sounding sinister and selfish, but rather joyous and selfless. They laughed and danced on the grass while butterflies fluttered around them.

The river became the warm Atlantic Ocean and sea water surrounded her feet, making her toes sink into the warm sand. Tony's eyes grew serious and his lips touched hers. The weight of the engagement ring felt like a kettle bell on her finger.

Lost in each other, they fell onto the blanket that suddenly appeared on the sand at their feet. His mouth felt gentle, loving, glorious. Her hands moved in lazy patterns across his back, feeling the hard muscles, loving his strength. He raised his head and smiled down at her, and she saw the need inside her reflected in his eyes.

"You know what I want, Robin." Tony said.

"Tony, I can't," She whispered.

Tony stared at her, his jaw set. "You named your price and I paid it. You know what I want."

"Tony," she begged. "Tony, no."

"I always get what I want."

Robin clawed her way out of the nightmare, bolting into a sitting position on the bed. Her whole body quaked in the aftermath. Her hands trembled and her breath came in quick shaky gasps. Sweat poured over her body, and she lifted the damp tendrils of her bangs to wipe her forehead.

She drew her legs up and rested her forehead against her knees. Her breathing slowly returned to normal. Her hands slowly stopped shaking, and the sweat cooled on her body. She stayed where she sat, waiting for the effects of the dream to fade away. She didn't want to carry the cobwebs of the nightmare out of the room with her and into the presence of her sisters.

CHAPTER ELEVEN

Robin clutched the bag in her hand a little tighter as the elevator came to a stop. She stepped out into the lobby of Tony's executive offices. The receptionist was speaking into her headset, so she just lifted her hand in a greeting and walked to Tony's office.

Her stomach twisted itself into painful knots, and she could barely breathe. As she got closer to the double doors leading to his outer office, she felt like they lay suddenly farther away. A cold sweat broke out on her upper lip.

She'd dressed carefully this morning, choosing a long navy blue pencil skirt and gray cashmere sweater. Now she wished she'd worn something cooler, or maybe layers so she could shed some heat. Thankfully, she'd thought to pin her hair up, so at least that wasn't suffocating her.

She noticed the tremble in her hand as she opened the door and stepped into Margaret's office.

Margaret stood as Robin entered." Hello, Robin. Mr. Viscolli will be happy to see you," she said, moving around her desk to open the large door leading to Tony's inner sanctuary.

Not for long, she thought, but merely smiled and put a shaking hand to her stomach.

Tony stood next to his desk, sorting papers. His suit jacket was draped on the chair behind him. He wore a white shirt with a blue and black striped tie. When he looked up, he had a distracted frown on his face, but when his eyes met Robin's, his features immediately relaxed and he smiled.

"*Cara mia*," he said, setting the stack of papers down and coming around his desk. "What an unexpected pleasure. Nothing could have surprised or pleased me more."

Robin did not hear Margaret shut the door behind her. Her heart started pounding and nausea churned in her gut. As Tony walked forward, she had to resist the urge to step backward. When he was just a few feet away from her, he did not step any closer, nor did he reach out to her.

"What happened?" he asked, his eyes searching her face.

Robin gripped the twine handle of the bag so tightly that she was surprised it didn't cut her skin. "Can we sit?" She gestured at the leather sofa.

"Yes. Of course. Are you ill? What's wrong?" Tony put a hand on her elbow as they moved to the sitting area. Robin fought the urge to lean into him and let him make everything okay. When she was with him, it seemed like it would definitely always be okay. But in her heart, she knew that was a false sense of security.

He sat on the couch, and she perched on the edge of the couch, turning her body toward him. With a shaking hand, she wiped the sweat off of her lip. "I—" Her breath hiccupped, but she forced forward and refused to give in to tears. If she cried, he would put his arms around her, and she would lose all strength to go forward with this.

He reached for her hand, sandwiching it between both of his. "Your hands are freezing," he said, concerned.

"Tony," she whispered, "I can't marry you."

She kept eye contact, despite a desire to look away. She watched the emotions play across his face, watched as concern mixed with confusion and a little bit of panic. "I don't understand. What are you saying?"

"I've been so stressed about it. I can't be Mrs. Viscolli. I can't do the cars and the trips and the jewelry. I can't plan a wedding that has a governor and three senators attending. I can't be that person. It's not me. I'm just a bartender who didn't even graduate from high school." She could hear the frantic tone of her own voice. "That reporter, he knew the truth about me. Everyone will know the truth about who I really am."

Understanding replaced the panic in his eyes. "Robin, if we go into this together, we can do or be anything. They are just people, just names. God loves them equally to the beggar on the street."

"They expect a certain class, certain knowledge and understanding. I don't have that. Your world has rules and expectations I don't even know about. I can't—"

"I love you. God made me for you and you for me. Nothing else should matter."

Swallowing the tears that burned the back of her eyes she said, "I love you, too. Passionately and forever. But that doesn't fix it. I know I will be inadequate as your wife. You deserve someone better suited to that role. You deserve the best."

He lifted her hands and pressed a kiss against her wrist. She knew he could feel the skittering of her pulse. "You are one of the smartest people I've ever met. You can learn, just like I learned, how to maneuver through certain crowds, how to handle yourself."

"I don't want to learn," she said, barely above a whisper.

He released her hand and framed her face, tilting her head toward his and searching her eyes. "What else? Something else. What is it?"

Panic crowded her brain, cutting off her breathing, taking away her ability to think straight. Heart pounding, she pushed his hands away and stood, rubbing her palms on her hips. "I don't—"

Tony stood with her. Despite the heels on her boots, he felt taller than her. "*Spiegati*," he said, anger seeping into his voice. "Don't just flip some excuse at me and expect me to fall for it. You explain. Whatever it is, I can fix it. We can fix it. You must tell me what it is."

Wrapping her arms around herself, she cleared her throat. "I had a bridal shower last night."

Tony gave a barely imperceptible nod. "I know."

"I got this set of—" Robin waved her hand in the air. "—wedding night… things. Silk, lace."

He slipped his hands into his pockets, but she saw him ball them into fists. "Go on."

"It suddenly occurred to me what marrying you would mean. I mean, it's not like I didn't intellectually know before. But it never really hit me before."

"What it would mean?" He frowned. "You mean sex?"

"The thought—" Defeated, she slumped down into a chair, gripping her hands in her lap. "My mom had some boyfriends who—"

Tony knelt at her feet and put his hands on top of hers. "You told me that before, remember?"

"I hinted, I know. But I haven't told you. I haven't told you about the horror, the pain, the disgusting—" she swallowed, trying to keep from getting sick. "The humiliation. You can't know what it was like. Not being strong enough, not being smart enough. Just enduring."

She ripped her hands away from his and pushed to her feet. The bag sat on the table in front of the couch. "I can't marry you. I can't be some billionaire's wife, and I can't be who you need me to be in the bedroom. Marrying me, despite how much I long to be yours forever, would be horribly unfair for you." She pointed at the bag. "That has the jewels you've given me, the sapphire necklace and the ruby heart. It also has the car keys in it." Slipping off her sapphire engagement ring, she set it on the table next to the bag. "I wish I were different. I wish I could wipe my memory like Sarah and just not remember anything. But, I can't. I'm not going to tie you to me. You deserve so much better than a broken bride."

He hadn't moved from his spot on the floor next to the chair. He did not reach out to her nor try to stop her as she walked across the office and out the door. No tears fell as she waved good-bye to Margaret.

The ride down the elevator took just as long as the ride up but felt like decades. She halfway expected security to meet her at the bottom and escort her back to Tony's office, but she reached the lobby without incident and walked through, not even seeing the people whom she knew who greeted her.

She held the tears in check until she found herself seated in the subway and, as the train pulled away, the first sob nearly ripped her in two.

TONY felt trapped. He didn't know how long he knelt next to that chair. He didn't know how long it took for him to start breathing again, for the fist that clutched his chest so painfully to release its grip long enough to let him inhale and exhale.

He leaned forward and rested his forehead against the chair. He intended to pray, but no words came. Instead, he closed his eyes and just tried to stop the onrush of maddening thoughts—tried to still his racing mind.

How could he fix this? What could he do? He couldn't go back in time. The man who raped her was already dead. There was no closure there. He couldn't change that situation. How to fix this?

Powerless. Helpless. Impotent.

After an endless time of being unable to even talk to God, he shakily stood to his feet. Feeling like he was suffocating, he loosened his tie and unbuttoned the top button of his shirt. He paced to his window that overlooked Boston's business district. All the power and influence that money could buy lay at his fingertips, and everything he'd worked for and accumulated for so long, laying one brick atop another day after day, was the wall that separated him from his happiness. His wealth and her past conspired to keep Robin from wanting to be with him.

A swift knock on his door interrupted his thoughts simultaneously with the sound of his intercom buzzing. Impatient, resentful at the intrusion, he turned around as Barry Anderson and Abram Rabinovich entered his office.

He rubbed his eyes with one hand then pinched the bridge of his nose. "Not now," he said.

"Ah, but we have an appointment," Abram said, smiling around his bearded face. "We are meeting for lunch to discuss building a new playground at the low income daycare."

"Just build it. Build whatever you want," he said, turning back to look out the window. Through gritted teeth he murmured, "Send me the bill."

"Hey. What's wrong?" Barry asked, setting his briefcase on the chair in front of Tony's desk. "What happened?"

Tony shoved his hands into his pockets. "My beloved fiancée has just called off our wedding a mere two weeks before the happy day," he said, strangling around the words.

"What?" Abram put a hand on Tony's shoulder. "Did something happen?"

Tony gave a harsh laugh. "Yeah, I'm worth a fortune. And I'm a man. Apparently, those two things are working against me."

Barry slapped a hand on his other shoulder almost knocking Tony off balance and squeezed. They stayed like that for a while and Barry asked, "How do you feel about it?"

Tony reached up and squeezed the bridge of his nose, shutting his eyes tight. With a deep breath, he said, "I feel like a failure. A complete failure."

Barry said, "Let's talk it out, brother. Listen, it's possible she did you a favor. Better to know now than when it's too late, right?" Tony whipped his head around and glared at Barry. But the giant did not even flinch. "Come on, Tony. Don't look at me like you have no idea what I'm talking about. You're my best friend, so you never bring it up, but you know."

Abram put his arm all the way over Tony's shoulder, subtly yet not so subtly knocking Barry's hand off. "My friend, I know you're a prayerful person and Robin has been the center of your prayer life for many months, now.

If the Holy Spirit is commanding you and directing you to make her your wife, who are you to ignore those commands?"

"I'm not the one ignoring anything. She came to me. She said she couldn't be Mrs. Viscolli. She said she couldn't interact with the people in my circles, that they'd see through to her background and she'd never measure up."

Abram nodded. "She likely has a point. Imagine how intimidating all this is to her. You're asking her to sacrifice everything she knows—her entire life. She has to change everything from her address to her name. Marriage is supposed to mirror our relationship with Christ." He led Tony across the large expanse of the room to the couch and guided him to sit down. "When I became a believer, I was disowned by my family. My father can barely even look at me, and to this day, I have a sister who refuses to acknowledge that I exist. And I lost everything. Everything. But, for Christ, I gave it all up."

Abram stopped speaking and just stared passively into Tony's eyes, as if waiting for Tony to say something, except Tony had no idea what to say. He didn't want to be rude and ask his mentor, "What's your point?" So he just nodded.

Abram shook his head, knowing that Tony had missed the point. "Tony, what is God calling you to sacrifice?"

Tony considered that. His default was to try to figure out what he should do, not what he should let go. What had he sacrificed? Had he sacrificed anything since he had met Robin? What was he willing to sacrifice to show her that he knew they belonged together? In the middle of his thoughts, his intercom buzzed. "Mr. Viscolli, Miss Maxine

Bartlett is on the phone for you. You said to interrupt if she called today."

He cleared his throat before answering. "*Si. Grazie.*" He pushed off of the couch and crossed over to his desk. "Maxi. Hello."

"Tony," she said in a rush, "I'm so sorry to bother you. I just met with the contractor at my new place, and I was hoping I could come by and show you what he showed me. I want to make sure it's all on the up and up."

His mind rejected the idea of helping Maxine, but he had committed to her that he would help her in any way. She obviously did not know Robin's plans that morning, or she surely would not have even called him. Perhaps he could glean some insight into Robin's change of heart if he had a chance to talk with Maxine. "Please, come by," he said.

Tony buttoned his top button and straightened his tie. He held out his hand to Abram. "My brother, thank you. Your wisdom is a blessing to me."

"Call me if you need me."

Tony took a deep breath and released it. "Maybe ask Sofia—if she felt it was appropriate—for her to intervene on my behalf?"

"I will be happy to ask." Abram assured.

"Thank you."

He hugged Barry. "Thank you for your honesty."

Barry picked up his briefcase. "You know where to find me if you want to talk more. I'll be praying for you, brother."

MAXINE juggled a rolled up set of plans and a

notebook as she entered Tony's office. He met her at the door and gestured at the conference table "I know you're busy. Are you sure you don't mind me barging in like this?" She placed the paperwork on top of the table and turned and looked him in the face. Red rimmed eyes stared at the door behind her. "Wait. What's wrong?"

Tony took a step backward. "I—"

The look of panic gave away more than his lack of warmth and lack of greeting combined. "No. Something's wrong. What's wrong?"

Tony rubbed the back of his neck. "Robin—" His voice hitched.

"Robin what?" Nervous, panicked butterflies leapt to life in her stomach.

"She broke off the engagement this morning."

Shocked, Maxine felt her mouth drop open. She felt her spine straighten and she asked, "What did she say?"

Tony's face hardened so that his eyes conveyed absolutely no emotion. It surprised her when she looked at him in that moment. She barely recognized him. He raised an eyebrow. "She tried to play it off that it's about the money—" he said, but Maxine interrupted him.

"Actually, that's been a big deal for her this entire time. She's seriously struggling with it."

For a moment, his mask slipped and she could see the pain in his eyes before he snapped it back into place. "Right," he said, clearing his throat, "and she's scared about our wedding night."

"Your wedding night?"

His cheeks tinged pink and he rocked on his heels. "Sex," he said in a low voice.

Memories assaulted her, making her involuntarily flinch and back up a step. She ended up with her back against the wall. Tony stepped forward, hand up, as if to help her, but she put up her own hand. "No, don't touch me," she said, putting a hand on her heart. "Just give me a second."

"Maxi," Tony said, stepping a little closer to her than she could stand. The desolation in his voice, the unshed tears in his eyes, almost made her want to hug him and comfort him. "Help me to help her."

"I don't know if you can," she said, emotions swirling, requiring pencil and paper or paint for their release. She struggled with what—with how much—to say. "I don't know if he was the first, but as far as I know, he was the last. And, she fought him every single time. She never made it easy for him, and he'd punch her or hurt her until she was subdued and he could—" She put her hands on her cheeks. "—for months and months. Our mom knew and hated Robin for it. She'd hit her, scream at her, threaten to sell her to the highest bidder. It was hell. We lived in hell." She sighed. "I don't know how you can help her."

Tony cleared his throat and closed his eyes. A single tear escaped and slid down his cheek and he took an angry swipe at it and cleared his throat again. "Okay. Thank you," he whispered. He took a step back and opened his eyes. "Can we talk about this another time?" he asked, gesturing at his conference table.

"Oh, what, this? Yeah, sure. I'll go. I'm so sorry, Tony." Mind whirling, she gathered her purse from under a notebook.

"*Grazie.*"

She turned to leave, but turned back. He was already headed back toward his desk. "Tony?" He paused but did not turn. She could see his shoulders shaking with the emotion he contained. "I love you. You are an amazing man and I'm thankful you're in our lives. But, I love her more."

Tony's shoulders suddenly slumped. Maxine went on, "I can't see her get hurt. I'll back whatever play she feels like she needs to make. If that means things have to change between you and me right now, then I understand."

His nod was very brief, but she saw it. She turned and left the office, desperate to go find her sister.

ROBIN sat on the front row of the small chapel affiliated with her church. She'd gone in here because she didn't want to walk into the main building and encounter anyone she knew. This chapel was a one-room structure used for small weddings and small funerals. She had come to pray, but she didn't know what to say, so she just poured her heart out to God with sobs while her mind swirled with thoughts of Tony, the love he'd shown her, the patience and understanding he'd given her. She thought of the joy in his eyes whenever he'd give her some stupidly expensive gift. Her heart ached at the thought of not being with him anymore.

She couldn't get over the look on Tony's face, the absolute helplessness. She wanted to go to him and take it all back and let him put the ring back on her finger, but she couldn't. The thought of conceding and what that meant she'd have to face—she just couldn't do it.

"Please God," she said, "help me. Guide me in this."

She heard the door open and she turned her head, startled. It partially surprised her and partially annoyed her when Sofia and Caroline came through the door.

The two pastors' wives could not look more

different—Sofia in her trim camel colored suit perfectly coifed, Caroline in her blue jeans and flannel shirt with her red hair sticking out everywhere. Robin could not love either woman more but she felt she needed solitude and privacy just now. They marched right up to her and then sat on each side of her making it clear they were here to stay. Caroline took her hand and Sofia put her arm over her shoulders.

Giving in, Robin rested her head on Sofia's shoulder and sobbed. "I—"

"Hush, love," Caroline said, "just let it out." She handed Robin a cotton handkerchief, and Robin sobbed into it until it was soaked with sweat and tears. When she finally felt like she could cry no more, she closed her eyes and willed the headache to fade away.

"I called Stephanie Giordano," Sofia said. "She had not heard from you yesterday or today. That tells me you didn't cancel plans, and *that*, my very young child, tells me that you do not *want* to cancel plans."

Robin's sigh shuddered out of her body. "Of course I don't want to cancel any plans. In the midst of destroying the most amazing man on the planet, I simply forgot to call my wedding planner. I'll get on it right away."

Caroline ran her hand over Robin's hair. "Do you know why I don't have any children of my own?" she asked, her Irish voice lyrical and overwhelmingly comforting. Robin shook her head. "Because a man hurt me when I was far too young. It was actually a miracle I even lived. But I did, though the doctors in Dublin told my mother that I'd likely never have children. Turns out they were right."

Robin felt the air leave her body. "I'm so sorry," she whispered.

"I have had decades to heal," she said, "and the love of a good man. It wasn't easy trusting him, but I'm so very, very glad I did. I may never have known the special and private beauty God, in His incredible wisdom, has given husbands and wives."

"God created a perfect planet," Sofia said. "Then Eve took of the fruit, Adam took the fruit from her, and it broke the perfection. The world is groaning from the weight of sin. What God originally designed is not what is today." She hugged Robin. "God's nature is contrary to the violence that you, and so many others, have experienced."

Caroline interjected. "Tony's past is filled with women who abandoned him. Women who were supposed to take care of him, and love him, and nurture him, and protect him. Instead, at too young of an age, he had to take up for himself. His past is riddled with drugs and abuse, and the only love he could find was the momentary kind that he occasionally paid for, much to his present shame."

"God has given you to Tony as much as He has given Tony to you. You two can heal each other and become one together. Not just physically, but spiritually as well," Sofia said.

"I don't know how——" Robin said, her voice hitching.

Caroline interrupted. "As comfortable as you are with Tony, just holding hands, talking, laughing, kissing, a physical relationship beyond that will be just as loving and fulfilling." She put a hand on Robin's wet cheek. "I know this, love. I live it. You can't imagine it because you've never known it. But I tell you, child, I mourn for your loss if you never know it."

Robin put her elbows on her knees and laced her fingers, resting her forehead against her hands. "What if it's not?"

Sofia ran a hand over her hair. "It will be. But if there is a problem, you simply pray together. Everything will work out. God brought the two of you together, and He will work it out."

"Let's pray together now," Caroline said. "We'll pray for you to have wisdom and we'll pray that your heart not be troubled and be strengthened for the path ahead."

CHAPTER TWELVE

errick DeNunzio sat outside Tony Viscolli's office wearing black slacks, a white button down shirt, and a waiter's vest. He was proud of his clean, crisp uniform.

He tried to start seeing himself through Tony's eyes. Tony had seen something in Derrick from the first time they met. Derrick had run out of options in his old life. He was miles underwater and drowning before Tony had thrown him a lifeline. Derrick had grabbed it and was hanging on by his fingernails and toes. He determined that he would work hard for Tony, show the man what he could do.

Derrick discovered that, for maybe the first time in his life, he was actually applying himself very tactically to a present path of work and personal sacrifice in order to strategically accomplish future goals in a committed way. That commitment and that personal hard work and sacrifice made him realize something even more shocking. He figured out that this new feeling he had been feeling since he decided to follow this path was a feeling he had never before had any reason to feel. He felt proud of himself and he felt valued and valuable.

But in the last few weeks, something had been on his mind more and more. Something he couldn't wrap his head around—or his heart. Or maybe his soul, he wasn't sure. It was something and he didn't really have anyone else he could talk to about it so he had made a breakfast appointment with Tony.

Tony arrived at 8:15 and Derrick found himself standing, unconsciously balancing his weight on the balls of his feet out of years of pure habit. He nodded a greeting to Derrick and said, "Margaret, could you please have the kitchen send up something hot for the two of us. Maybe some hot bagels and some cream cheese, too. No hurry."

Tony turned back to Derrick and gestured that the younger man should precede him into his office. Having worked the nightshift and not having seen Tony for a few days despite living in his apartment, Derrick said, "Good morning, sir."

"Just getting off?" Tony asked.

"Yes. It's a long shift until eight." Derrick's muscles felt slightly fatigued just from battling his body's desire to sleep.

They settled down on the couches as they had the very first time Derrick had ever come to this office. Tony remained silent, letting the young man collect his thoughts, lost in his own. Four days had gone by since Robin visited him, and he felt like he was trapped in a swirling abyss. He simply did not know what to do next. The only thing, and it was truly the only thing, that kept him moving forward day after day was the fact that everyone in his employ involved in this wedding still thought Robin was going through with it. Robin hadn't canceled anything yet. He still had hope.

It almost took them both by surprise when, after a few minutes of silence, the breakfast arrived. Tony let Derrick pour them coffee, noticing the ear marks of Derrick's waiter training as the young man set the cups 'just so' and arranged the silverware to the Viscolli Boston standard on the cloth napkins to the right of each plate.

When Derrick didn't touch his food or drink, Tony finally spoke again. "Why don't I bless this meal and then you tell me why you called this meeting, Derrick." It wasn't a question.

Derrick nodded. Tony blessed their meal and sipped his coffee as Derrick began to speak. Tony pushed aside all thoughts of Robin, knowing he needed to be all there for Derrick.

"Mr. Viscolli, I have to tell you something. The other day when we was, I mean, when we were helping Robin and her sisters move, you were telling Robin and them that you knew I didn't steal anything. You know, those jewels. Her jewelry. I don't know if you know, but I heard you. I was just outside her bedroom door, in the hallway, and I heard you."

Tony pursed his lips. "That's fine, Derrick. I didn't say anything I wouldn't have said in front of you."

"I know, Mr. Viscolli. I just…" His voice suddenly stopped working. Derrick found himself in a surprisingly awkward and precarious state. There was a giant lump in his throat that his words couldn't get around and he couldn't breathe past it either. He felt tears welling up in his eyes and he suddenly hung his head in shame when he realized that he was about to break down and cry in front of this man.

As unmanly and silent tears streamed down his face, he felt a strong hand grip his shoulder. "What is it, *figlio*? Tell me what is bothering you so." Tony urged.

Derrick gasped a baritone sob and heard silverware tumble as he grabbed his cloth napkin and covered his nose and mouth. Tony just kneaded the younger man's shoulder and somehow, someway, Derrick knew that the older man had started praying for him in that second.

After perhaps half a minute, Derrick's thick voice found its way out again. "No one has ever spoken up for me like that before. No one. Not even my mama." His voice vanished into three breathy, strangled sobs. Through gritted teeth, he said, "You have everything and I can't do anything for you. I looked around my room and realized something last night. I got almost nothing you didn't give me. Even the room you gave me. And I got nothing worth anything that you didn't. I don't understand this. I don't understand you. Why would you take up for me like that with them? How did you know I didn't steal that stuff?"

"Ahh." Tony clapped his hand on Derrick's shoulder. "Okay. I understand. I've been waiting for this, actually."

Tony walked over to the bookshelf behind his desk. He opened a file cabinet drawer and pulled out a miniature board game. It was a travel sized edition of the game of *Monopoly* and Derrick had a serious moment of doubt, wondering what a multi-billionaire was doing with a kid's game in his desk drawer.

"You know how to play this game?" He asked casually.

"I played a few times as a kid."

Tony met his eyes, "Ever win?"

Derrick shrugged. "I dunno. Maybe."

"Well, tell me this, how do you win this game?"

Derrick sat up. "I buy some properties and charge rent when you land on my property."

Tony nodded. "While that is a stunning display of your economic grasp of *lassais faire* capitalism, charging rent doesn't mean you win. What if I charge you higher rent when it's my turn? That's just how you play, right? Not how you win."

"Well, I can use the rent you pay me to build houses and then I collect higher rent. Then I can buy hotels."

Tony held up a little red hotel and then put it down on New York Avenue. "You mean a hotel like this one?" Somehow Derrick understood that Tony wasn't talking about the little plastic hotel game piece, but maybe he was actually referring to a hotel like the one in which they presently found themselves, or the Viscolli Hotel in Manhattan, or Atlanta, or Dallas, or Seattle, or Los Angeles. "Then you win?"

"No, it's a really long game. I would have to build houses and lots of hotels and eventually force you to sell and mortgage all your houses and hotels and properties and then I would have to buy them from you." Derrick said. "Then I would have to charge you rent until I took your very last dollar. Then I win. I win when you are flat broke."

Tony nodded and moved all the little dollar bills from his side of the board over to Derrick's side. Then he picked up the little hotel and set it on top of the pile of toy money. "Then you win."

Derrick nodded.

"So you are saying that now, when everyone else but you is flat broke, this is the end of the game. Okay. What did you learn? What did the game teach you? You own all the properties and railroads and houses and hotels and you even have yourself a get out of jail free card, maybe. So what did you learn in your rush to acquire absolutely everything and take away my very last dollar?"

Derrick sat back and looked at all the play money and the little red hotel sitting on his side of the board. "That if I work really hard, I can succeed?"

Tony nodded and stacked his empty dishes back on the rolling cart beside him. "What you say is true, Derrick, but it is not the most valuable lesson this game can teach you. I think I will give you one more try and then I will just tell you the answer."

Derrick searched his mind before he said, "I'm sorry. I don't know."

"I will tell you. The most important thing to learn is that now, it all goes back in the box." As he returned the items to the box, Tony continued. "See, you thought you owned all the properties and railroads and houses and hotels and your get out of jail free card. But now they go back in the box. Maybe you start to realize they were never even yours in the first place. They were there in the box long before you had them. Someone else owned them all before you did. And pretty soon, maybe someone else will come along and play with them after you're gone. All those houses you were so proud of. All the utility companies and rail lines. And all the wonderful, wonderful money. It all goes back in the box."

Tony put the lid on the box and said, "Now look around you. Tell me something. When you realize that the game isn't over when you have everything, when you realize the game isn't even over when you put everything back in the box—when you realize that—answer this question: what is *really* important?"

Tony stood and began to pace. He spoke low and deep, his voice quiet so that Derrick strained to hear his every word. "Maybe you get out the box again and you get all those properties and hotels and all that wonderful money back. Maybe. Or maybe you leave it all in the box and you realize what is really, really important in this life are not the things in there. What matters in this life is, in fact, much bigger than anything inside the box."

Tony stopped pacing and turned, his eyes boring into Derrick's eyes. "Because ultimately, everything you see and touch and consume in this world, all of it... even your own body... all of it goes back in the box one day."

Derrick sat back, his mind racing.

"Listen to me very carefully and I'll tell you about a gift that isn't inside the box. From this moment on, if you choose to accept this gift, your entire life will be very, very different. Do you want this gift? Because I am going to tell you something. Derrick, one day you will die. Everyone will. I will. You will. Your mother will. Everyone will. You are going to live and then you are going to die. And you are going to be dead a lot longer than you ever lived. That is the way it is. It is just that black and white. Now, when your life ends, when everything you owned in life gets put back in the box, you will suddenly find yourself on the outside of the box standing in front of that very same God who made you, and you will have to explain the choices you made while you played the game.

"See outside of this little game is you and me. Just like outside of here is the whole universe—and it is all just a box, Derrick. Outside of that box, my very young friend, is what is really, really important. Outside of all that is your Creator, God, Jehovah, A'doni, who is what He is, the great I AM.

"The truth is, you could have spent your life the way you had been living. You could have wasted your life away with drugs, pornography, gambling, thuggery, and spent your precious few remaining days and nights in the company of evil men and women—then died. But you knew that wasn't what you wanted. You didn't know this, but I was praying for you. I prayed for you every day. And then on the day after your birthday, you came to me and accepted the earthly gifts I had to offer. But your life still isn't what it could be, is it? Do you want it to be? Do you want to reach your full potential even if it means you will radically change?"

Derrick didn't realize that he was even speaking until the sound of his voice echoed in his own ears, "Yes."

Tony turned and said, "Good. Now I think you're ready for that gift I promised you." He knelt in front of Derrick. Derrick suddenly realized that his cheeks were wet with silent tears. "Do you believe in God, Derrick?"

Derrick barely recognized his own voice, "Yes."

Tony nodded, both of his hands holding Derrick's right hand. "And do you know what's important to that very same God you confess you believe in?"

Derrick shook his head.

"What's important to Him, more than anything else, is you. You, Derrick DiNunzio. You are the most precious thing in the universe to the Creator of the universe. You feel overwhelmed by the fact that I, a man, love you enough to stand up for you the way I did? That notion reduces you to tears? That I love you enough to take you in and feed you when you are hungry, clothe you when you are cold and exposed, pray for you when you are struggling with addiction and a life of crime? You feel overwhelmed by one man's love for you? Imagine how much God loves you.

"He loves you so much that He would actually lay

down his very life for you and die for you. In fact, He already did. He sent His only begotten son, Yeshua, called Jesus of Nazareth, as a living sacrifice in atonement for everything you have ever done wrong in this life. Do you believe that Derrick? Do you believe in Jesus Christ, that He was born of a virgin, lived a life that was pure, suffered under Pilate, and died for you? That on the third day He rose from the dead, conquering the grave, in testimony to the truth of his godhead?"

"Yes." Derrick whispered.

Tony said, "Then all you have to do now is accept that gift. You have so many things in your heart and mind that make you feel unworthy of love, but Derrick, you are worthy. You are worthy, Derrick. You are not here by accident. God created you on purpose. He knew you before He knitted you in your mother's womb. He loved you even then. The reason I wanted you to come to church with me was to educate you about God's love, about what the real love offered by the Creator of the universe can do. God loves you so much that His love can move mountains. And God tells me that I have to love you just as much. *Capisci?*

"So what you must do is just let go. Let go of your game. Open your hands. Let Jesus Christ rule your life. Bow down before him and accept the gift of His atoning blood that wipes the slate clean. Give up the stranglehold you have on your personal selfish hopes and desires, and turn your life over to a life of service in His name. Commit that you will stand for him even if you stand alone. Open your grasping hands and arms wide, as Christ did on the cross, and He will fill your empty arms with purpose and love and abundant life."

In the very next heartbeat, in the privacy of that very

well appointed office, in the company of Tony Viscolli, the most unlikely event took place. Derrick finally understood the overwhelming truth. In the space of a heartbeat, all of the puzzles and riddles that had plagued him for weeks clicked into place. When the weight of his past life fell from his heart, for the first time his life opened up. Where he had existed in constant agonizing torture inside an emotional iron maiden, he suddenly knew freedom. Where he had lived a life of simple survival in unbearable pain and darkness, he suddenly saw light and hope. In his heart of hearts, he heard a voice, his own voice it seemed, assuring him that everything would be all right. Yes, he would face struggles and adversity, but it would all work out fine. And Derrick, for the first time ever, believed it.

In the space of that heartbeat, the dying creature the world knew as Derrick DiNunzio went ahead and died and a brand new living creature named Derrick DiNunzio rose in its place. From that very next heartbeat, the Holy Spirit would guide the new Derrick not to see himself as others did, but rather as God saw him. The scales fell from his eyes. He would no longer judge the unimportant things in life as overly relevant, but rather see what really mattered and fight to make a difference. And he would love his neighbor the way God loved him.

CHAPTER THIRTEEN

Robin nearly felt her heart explode when she saw her photograph on the cover of *Inside Boston* magazine. A messenger had delivered this advance copy just before noon. The magazine would hit newsstands all over the city tomorrow morning. Not only had they given her the entire cover, they had selected what looked like a candid shot of Robin wearing a knee length skirt and matching jacket with a light blue blouse. In the picture, her unsmiling face looked speculative, confident, wise, and secure—pretty much the opposite of how she actually felt. Her crossed arms framed the engagement ring perfectly against the navy sleeve of her jacket. The headline read, *Millionaire Marries Manager*.

In the time since she had last seen Tony, Robin had neglected a few things. For example, she had neglected to inform another living soul that she would not, in fact, be marrying Tony Viscolli. She could not imagine how calling off the wedding would hurt Tony's public image. If she let herself think about it too much, she might burst into tears again so she stopped her racing thoughts in their tracks and opened the magazine.

> *Inside Boston's* intrepid reporter Don Roberts had the rare opportunity to sit down with Robin Bartlett. Robin manages Hank's Place restaurant which recently became one of Viscolli Enterprises newest acquisitions. It's unlikely that Tony Viscolli knew when he purchased the local eatery that the love of his life would come with the deal.
> While Tony Viscolli is as well known for his clout in the boardroom as his beneficence to Boston's less fortunate and his generosity to so many worthy charitable causes, Robin is very far from the blue blood debutante many might expect. In fact, just like her future husband, Robin came from humble beginnings right here in Boston. Despite her untraditional childhood, Robin Bartlett is sweet and smart, the kind of "girl next door" every Boston boy hopes to bring home to meet mom and dad one day. We asked Robin some questions about the upcoming wedding and her expectations for married life as the wife of one of Boston's royal family.

Some of the information she skimmed came straight out of Stephanie's press release with dates, places, names of designers and dress makers, jewelers, entrées and dinner courses, hors d' oeuvres and desserts, and even florists. Her canceled wedding was laid bare on the pages for the world to see in every excruciating detail except for the one minor detail: that it would never happen.

She skimmed the article down to the interview questions.

> IB: You two come from opposite ends of the financial spectrum. How do you feel about marrying one of the wealthiest bachelors in Boston?
> Robin: He is amazing and generous and loving, and I feel so incredibly blessed.

She remembered saying those words during the first interview, the one that concluded with security guards turkey trotting Don Roberts from the building. She skimmed further down.

> IB: Robin, so many things about your childhood would astonish our readers. From what you've shared with us, it was pretty rough. Your father was in prison. Your mother died of gunshot wounds. For part of your childhood, you were in the foster system. Anything you want to share with our readers about that?
> Robin: One of the things I admire about Tony is his heart for children. He supports hundreds of homes like the one here at Boston Bible that give children like my sisters and I once were a clean, safe, loving environment. I can't wait to support him in those ministries as his wife.

He had taken her answer out of context but somehow it fit perfectly. She spotted her father's name and read carefully.

> IB: Your father, Craig Bartlett, has been the topic of a number of news stories in recent months. What can you tell our readers about your dad?
>
> Robin: The Craig Bartlett of today, the man I know is not the man in the tabloid stories. My father turned himself in and confessed to all of his crimes without even trying to strike a deal. He is doing what he can to make restitution for his past wrongs. The way he has turned his life around despite his past, I have to say I'm proud of him. I pray for him every day.

It was a direct quote, what she had said word for word, but again out of context. Is this how interviews were supposed to be written?

> IB: Robin, in your opinion, what is the most attractive thing about Tony Viscolli?
>
> Robin: His abiding and unshakable faith in God and his faithfulness to Him is certainly the most attractive thing about my fiancé.
>
> IB: Your faith is important to you and your future husband. How would you characterize your beliefs?
>
> Robin: We're Christians.

She remembered how negatively Don Roberts had treated anything she had said about faith. Yet here, he highlighted their faith in the way that she wanted it seen by the world.

> IB: What do you think is your greatest
> accomplishment in your life, Robin?
> Robin: The greatest thing I've done in
> my life so far was getting custody of
> my sister, Maxine.
> IB: Any plans for after the wedding?
> Plan on doing a lot of shopping?
> Robin: I'll still run Hank's.

She read through all of the questions twice. The way that Don Roberts had combined answers from their initial and second interview into a cohesive article revealed every fact she had shared, but also put Robin Bartlett and Tony Viscolli in the best possible light.

When she turned the final page, she found a handwritten sticky note Don had left for her. In really minuscule print, he had written, "Robin, I realize Tony is a billionaire, not a millionaire, but it didn't have the same alliterative ring to it for the headline. You should know that I'm also a believer. I admire what the two of you are doing. The truth is you gave me a lot to think about, a lot to admire, and a lot to pray about. I wanted you to know that I am going to stop hiding my light under a bushel so much and let it shine a little more often. I pray I did you justice with this piece. Thanks for witnessing to me. Yours in Christ, DR."

The woman this *Inside Boston* article portrayed, from the photographs to the out of context quotations, was not the woman holding and reading the magazine. The woman within these pages was confident, competent, and capable. Magazine article Robin was accomplished, witty, polished, and professional. That Robin would certainly make a fine match for Tony Viscolli. She would love him and support him and make him happy throughout his lifetime.

By contrast, the very real Robin Bartlett had brought nothing but conflict, heartache, and shame to Tony Viscolli since the very day he had first laid eyes on her. Everything about her spelled trouble from her heritage, her violent past, her lack of education, to her ignorance of the day to day politics of the high society world in which he lived. She wondered how Don Roberts would handle the fact that the woman who had witnessed to him so profoundly was less than two weeks away from leaving Tony Viscolli at the altar.

This magazine would hit newsstands tomorrow. She could not fight that. She could not run from that. She could not hide from that. She envisioned her life spinning away and out of control, down into a bottomless vortex like a fast sinking ship. She envisioned taking Tony and dozens of others down along with her.

TONY stood in Barry's office, hands in his pockets, looking out at the courthouse. A copy of the most recent *Inside Boston* lay atop Barry's desk but both men had studiously ignored its presence there. Although neither mentioned it, both of them occasionally let their eyes stray back to glance at Robin Bartlett's photo on the cover.

"You're right. It isn't unethical or illegal. It's just completely unheard of." Barry ran his massive hand through his straw blond hair. "Tony, I can't do this."

"You must. I'm ordering you to," Tony said with a half grin that had nothing to do with humor.

Barry shook his head. "You must be of sound mind

and body to execute legal instruments of this nature. And clearly, you're just a little bit out of your mind right now," his friend observed.

"No, I'm not." Or, maybe Barry was right. Maybe Tony had lost his senses. Could it be that he was getting in the way of God's will for his life right now? Was he allowing greed, or pride, or anger to dictate or manipulate his actions? He really didn't think so. This felt exactly right. He had a lot of fear and he felt very angry that he could still feel fear, but outside of that was nothing except a sense of peace. "I'm really not crazy. I know what I'm doing."

Tony turned to look at his attorney and very best friend in the entire world and Barry shook his head again. "Do you have any idea what this will mean?"

"We can work it out to make it as simple as possible. But I'm serious about my timeline."

Barry sighed. "I don't think I can do this for you. Tony, I'm your lawyer but you and I are best friends. If you go through with this, what will happen to our friendship? You're the only person I can really even talk to anymore. I can't—"

Tony stepped forward and held up a finger. His voice became hard, like steel, and cold. He spoke as if to a subordinate, ensuring that Barry knew that friendship was on the line already. "You will do it, Barry, or else I'll find someone who will. Again, I'm not asking your opinion or your advice in this matter. I am simply hiring you to do a job and you will be paid very well to accomplish it."

Tony watched Barry's eyes flash, but felt no remorse at standing up to his best friend. "Fine," Barry bit. Then with practiced cordiality, "Please have a seat, Mr. Viscolli. Make yourself comfortable. Pardon my unprofessional outburst. I can ask Elizabeth to order up some lunch, if you like. We have quite a number of details to cover and this will take some time."

ROBIN tried to pay attention to whatever show Sarah had put on the television for them, but honestly, she couldn't focus. Tomorrow would be Tuesday, which means she destroyed her life and the life of the most amazing man on the planet just five short days ago. Since the day their relationship started, she hadn't ever gone so long without talking with him, without seeing him. Sunday she'd skipped church, afraid to go and be seen by him, or be seen with him. She could barely breathe. She felt lost, floundering, sinking, and had no idea what to do next.

She still hadn't told Maxine or Sarah. All evening, Sarah had excitedly talked about the shoes Maxine had found for them to wear with their bridesmaid dresses. How could she tell them? What could she say?

Now she sat limp on the edge of the couch staring at the television screen. She didn't even know what they were watching.

She heard Maxine's keys in the door. She barely looked up when her sister stormed into the apartment.

"All right. I've had enough. I've kept my mouth shut for nearly a week, waiting for you to come to me, and I'm tired of it." Maxine announced as she tossed her keys on a little table by the door. Sarah used the remote to pause the movie and looked between Robin and Maxine. "Are you planning to mention it to us?"

Robin glared at Maxine. She'd cried until she honestly didn't think she could cry anymore. Today she'd been kind of a zombie, stumbling around, not sure about what she should do, what she should wear, what she should eat. It took a moment to understand what Maxine was talking about. "No."

Maxine slammed the door, making Sarah jump. "What's going on?" the youngest sister asked.

"Robin here," Maxine said, "broke it off with Tony."

Sarah looked as confused as if Maxine had just announced that pigeons no longer flew, preferring instead to swim. "What?"

"Last Thursday."

"What?!" Sarah's head whirled around. "Robin? Why didn't you say something?"

Robin stood. "Because I don't want you two cooing over Tony and telling me how great he is, how great it is that I'm going to be his wife."

Sarah blinked. "But—"

Maxine stepped forward. "No, we won't. We are here to tell you we love you, and whatever you need from us, you'll get." She grabbed Robin and hugged her. "I understand." She pulled back and looked into Robin's eyes. Robin saw all of the pain and fear that she felt reflected back from her sister's emerald pools. "You know I understand. Whatever you need."

Tears fell from burning dry eyes literally worn out from crying. "Thank you," Robin whispered.

Sarah got up and hugged both Robin and Maxine. "Honey, I'm so sorry," she said. "What can I do?"

Robin closed her eyes, resetting back to last summer, to the way she thought, to her motivations then. "Graduate with honors and get a good job," she said. "That's all I've ever wanted from you."

Sarah reached out and put a tentative light hand on Robin's shoulder. "Did he, you know, did he do something?"

Robin shook her head slowly. "No." She sobbed as she said, "He didn't do anything. He didn't do anything at all. He is absolutely as wonderful as ever."

TONY shifted his portfolio in his hand and opened the door to Robin's office. For the briefest second, he had a chance to observe her working, head down, scribbling on a scheduling sheet in front of her. Then she looked up, and the distracted concentrated look abandoned her face, replaced with hesitation and apprehension. He prayed, as he had been praying all morning, that this went smoothly. Because, he honestly never wanted to see that look on her face when she looked at him ever again.

He stepped into the office and shut the door, reaching behind him to lock it. Robin leaned back in her chair and raised an eyebrow. "Is that to keep me in or others out?"

"*Qualunque*," he said with a shrug. At her blank look, he said, "Whichever."

Her eyes flashed and he watched her look at the door then at him. "I see."

He walked to her desk and set the portfolio on top of it. "I had Margaret call Stephanie today about RSVP's and just to—well, in general—to make small talk. Apparently, the wedding is still on."

Robin's cheeks turned red and she looked at the blotter in front of her. "I guess I should call and cancel. But—"

"But that seems final and extreme," he finished for her. "And very, very real." He pulled a piece of paper out of the portfolio.

Robin's eyes swam with tears. "I don't want this." Her

voice sounded raw. She ripped open the desk drawer and pulled out her tin of mints. Her hands trembled and it took her a second to open it and pop one into her mouth.

"But you want this?" he asked, tossing her two-week resignation notice onto the desk in front of her.

"Of course not," she said, pushing the paper toward him. "But I can't keep working for you, either."

"Why not?"

"Because I love you too much to constantly see you and talk to you, to work as your subordinate when I want nothing more than to be by your side."

Tony's heart skipped a furious beat in his chest. He took a deep breath and sat down. "I've never had a restaurant run with such love as what you give this place. I am here to ask you to reconsider quitting."

"I'm afraid that's out of the question." She leaned back in her chair and rested her elbows on the arm, clutching her pen with both hands. "I can't do it. It will hurt too much."

Tony pulled a stack of papers out of the case. "You won't need to worry about that," he said. He tossed them in front of her.

"What are these?" She leaned forward and picked up a packet, recognizing the layout of a legal court document.

"These," he said as he sat in the chair across from her, "are the documents to legally dissolve my stakes in all of my companies. I will sell shares, give some away, and hand over corporate responsibilities to someone else, depending on the company. Metaphorically, I'm putting this game back in the box. When these documents are executed I will be penniless and, in a few short months, homeless, too." He straightened his tie. "I started with nothing. I can certainly start over."

He said it all very matter-of-factly while his insides turned to a boiling mass of fear and emotion. "But I can only face something like that with you by my side, *cara*."

"What?" Robin furiously flipped through a packet of paper. "What are you talking about?"

"Well," Tony said, "you have an issue with my money and my status. So, I'll make those things a non-issue."

"What about your employees?"

"Obviously, some of them will need new employers."

Robin tossed the packet on top of her desk. "Is this some kind of joke?"

He narrowed his eyes and very dangerously said, "Why in the name of the most holy God would you think anything about this is a joke?"

"Because you sound very casual about something that should be much more important to you."

He was around the desk, gripping the arms of her chair with both hands and leaning down so that his face was close to hers before he even realized he was in motion. "This is one of the most important things in my life, I can assure you. But, as important as it is, you are a million times more important. Do you understand that?" He shook the chair so that it rattled. "Do you get that I would do anything for you? Sell off everything, become a penniless pauper, have a celibate marriage—anything I need to have you by my side."

Robin's breath hitched and she put her hand on her chest. "How do I—?"

Kneeling to take her hands with his, he gentled his voice. "My darling love, you tell me what to do. You tell me how to fix it so that you are willing to be with me. I don't need companies or money or things. But I need you."

Tears slid down her cheeks, breaking him into a million

pieces. "You can't disband Viscolli Enterprises," she said. "God uses it for too much good."

"Robin, that is exactly wrong. God does not need me. I need Him. And I assure you, He will find other ways to use us."

"No." Shredded pieces of Tony's heart landed at her feet at the finality of the tone in her voice. "No. You can't do that. There are ministries, shelters, orphanages. I can't be responsible for that." Tony bowed his head and closed his eyes. He rested his forehead on their joined hands, broken. "If you will make me a couple of promises, then maybe I can marry you."

It took a second for her words to penetrate the mist of desolation in his brain. As soon as he understood her, he looked up. "What promises?"

Robin took a deep shaky breath and brushed the hair on his forehead. He felt the tingle from the touch of her fingertips go down the nape of his neck. "I can't jump right in to your world. I need to gradually get my feet wet. Keep our social engagements to a bare minimum for at least a year."

"Done."

"Don't leave my side during a function and leave me floundering without you."

"*Cara*, I would not want to leave your side for any reason."

"I don't want to talk to any reporters without you."

"Already done."

As her eyes welled with fresh tears, she put a shaking hand on his cheek. "I'm so afraid of our wedding night. I can't even think straight. How will I get through the ceremony in front of all those people? How will I ever handle the reception and the small talk and hours of socializing knowing what waits for me?"

Tony reached forward and cupped her cheeks with his hands. "My darling, what horror of horrors waits for you is me. Robin, my beloved, I will never hurt you. You don't need to be afraid of me. But, I promise you, that everything will go at your pace and any time you want to stop, I will stop. Every time. As for the other, I have an idea."

CHAPTER FOURTEEN

At two p.m., Barry's phone chimed and he distractedly said, "Yes, Elizabeth?"

"Sir, Tony Viscolli is here to see you."

Intrigued, Barry slipped off his reading glasses and shut the lid of his laptop. "Send him in."

Tony never came to visit him. Barry always went to him. It didn't bother him because, after all, Tony was the client. In their personal meetings, they typically met outside of their individual offices. But their last meeting two days ago had taken place in this very office and ended with each of them feeling extremely tense. Barry wasn't even certain exactly where their friendship stood right now.

He pushed back from his desk and stood, slipping on his suit jacket as Tony came through the door. Tony carried a leather portfolio, but was dressed down in khaki slacks and a black cotton sweater. Barry could see the wet cuffs of his pants and knew Tony had spent the morning out on the water, rowing. He knew that was what Tony did to get completely away from all distractions and to think while his body worked the boat through the water. He also knew Tony chose that sport above all others because it was the sport of choice for the blue-bloods of this part of the country.

As Barry rounded his desk, his friend spoke first. "I owe you an apology for the way I spoke to you the last time we were together," he said.

Barry paused in the buttoning of his coat. He raised an eyebrow, but did not reply. Tony continued speaking. "I was extremely emotional at the moment and not quite acting myself."

Barry nodded. "Hence the whole 'are you sure you want to do this' question from me and the observation regarding your mental state."

"I understand. I needed to do it, but I understand why you questioned it and what you said." He opened the portfolio and pulled out a stack of papers. "Robin and I have reconciled." He set the papers on the conference table near him. "You can destroy these documents."

Barry waged an internal debate for about ten seconds before finally stepping forward. "Can we talk?"

"Of course," Tony said. He pulled out a leather chair from the table and sat, crossing his legs and brushing at his knee.

Barry sat next to him and said, "Tony, if there is even the most remote possibility of any issues with this marriage, I'm asking you as your best friend and your Best Man to reconsider it."

Tony raised an eyebrow. "Oh?"

Barry sighed. "We never really talk about this so I'm not sure how I should approach it. I'll just get this out of the way. Are you aware that my wife is often unfaithful? Are you aware that, as far as I know, she hasn't been faithful to me for at least the last six years?"

Tony kept his face perfectly schooled and nodded once, holding Barry's eyes with his own. He did not speak.

Barry seemed to relax a little bit, his enormous shoulders lowering as some tension left them. "For the longest time, I focused on the book of Hosea. I really am trying to do God's will in my marriage, Tony. The fact is, I love my wife and I intend to keep my vows even if she doesn't. But there is nothing worse than waking up in the morning, alone in my bed, knowing how much my wife despises me, and knowing there is absolutely nothing I can do about it because I've tried everything already."

Tony closed his eyes and took a deep breath, running a finger over his forehead. When he opened them again, Barry could read love, friendship, and sadness in them. "I don't know how you do it, Barry. But know that if there is anything at all I can do to help you, I wouldn't hesitate."

"I know," Barry said impatiently. "I've never doubted that. I just want to make sure you don't end up in a similar position as that in which I find myself. I thought I was marrying a princess who would be my queen. Instead I married a diva."

"Thank you for being candid." Tony sat forward. "Robin is coming from a background of abuse—mental, physical, and sexual—she's a poster child. It's incredible she survived her childhood. Her issues stem directly from that, not from—and understand I mean no disrespect to you in saying this—not from being an overindulged self-important diva."

Barry snorted and thought that it would be wrong to laugh. But he wanted to. "Okay. I think you should know that I really like Robin. I'm sorry that I might have ever given you any other impression. It's just that I don't want to end up seeing you hurt."

"Barry, thank you. For everything."

Barry grinned and teased, "Don't worry. I'll bill you for the hour."

Tony laughed. "Of that I have no doubt."

Barry schooled his features and said, "My prayer is that the two of you will be happy for the rest of your lives."

Tony stood and slapped his hand on Barry's shoulder. "That is my prayer for you as well, my friend."

JACQUELINE Anderson took a moment to lecture, "The purpose of the trousseau is to start your marriage off with a bunch of amazing clothes that you feel absolutely beautiful wearing."

She stood in the middle of the carpeted floor of the high end boutique on Newbury Street, just a short distance from Maxine's new apartment. She wore a royal blue pantsuit with a yellow and blue scarf and yellow high heeled shoes. Robin felt rather underdressed beside Barry's wife wearing her black slacks and a pink sweater with comfortable walking shoes. "If you feel beautiful in your clothes, you will naturally project beauty," Jacqueline said.

Robin nodded, understanding what the red head said. She currently felt frumpy and unattractive next to the stylish beauty.

"So, we need to see what styles work for you, then we'll pick out some outfits from there."

Jacqueline lifted her hand and the sales clerk came forward. "Mrs. Anderson, are we ready?"

"We are. Miss Bartlett, who will very soon be Mrs. Viscolli, needs to get an idea of what you offer, then we'll make some selections."

"Wonderful!" The clerk led them to some comfortable chairs. "Please have a seat here." She raised her voice slightly and said, "Ladies?"

From the back, a train of models walked through the small area in front of Robin and Jacqueline. Mirrors all around them showed the clothes they wore from all angles. Robin murmured to Jacqueline what she liked or didn't like about outfits, shoes, and accessories. When the show was over, Jacqueline took the lead and let the clerk know what else they wanted to see.

Two hours later, the clerk rang up the incomprehensibly expensive bill and Robin used the credit card Tony had given her that morning to satisfy the tab. She signed the receipt, arranged for the packages to be delivered to Tony's apartment, and assumed they were all done for the day. Until Jacqueline spoke and said, "Now, let's go two doors down. They have a fabulous new line."

"More?" Robin asked.

"Of course! We're starting with nothing. You have a whole month in front of you in Italy, darling. Six outfits from one store does not a full trousseau make!"

At the next shop, Jacqueline already had an idea of what Robin liked, so they didn't have to go through that learning experience again. Instead, they just shopped, bought, and shopped some more. Four stores and more money than Robin used to earn in a year later, they found themselves sitting across from one another in a trendy little cafe.

"That was an absolute blast," Jacqueline said, taking a delicate sip of her tea. "I haven't shopped on that scale in ages. Far too long, in fact."

Robin wished she could prop her feet up somewhere.

"I can't believe we just spent that much money on clothes," she said, picking up her coffee.

"You need a base. Your sister, what's her name? The one that's obviously mixed blood."

"Maxine." Robin tried not to feel resentment over the mixed blood remark. After all, it was true.

"Right. Maxine. She has great taste. I'm surprised she hasn't handled this for you."

Robin smiled. "Well, she would have loved to, but I wanted a chance to spend some time with you, too. After all, your husband and my soon-to-be husband are like brothers."

"Indeed," Jacqueline said, her mouth twisting in distaste.

"I assume we will spend a lot more time together."

"Honey, something about me and Bartholomew you should know is that we spend as little time together as possible. He and Antonio do all their stuff without me."

Robin frowned. "Why?"

"We just prefer it that way." She waved a dismissive hand. "But that doesn't mean we can't be friends, right? Mrs. Viscolli needs to know there are people she can count on to be her friends regardless of what her last name once was."

Robin pondered whether Jacqueline Anderson would even give her the time of day if she didn't currently sport an engagement ring from Tony Viscolli, but dismissed the negative thought. Whatever Jacqueline's motivations, Robin wanted to stay on friendly terms with her. She would hate having any bad feelings between the two of them as often as Tony and Barry were together.

CHAPTER FIFTEEN

Robin poured herself onto the couch. "Oh my heavens, I don't think I've ever felt so relaxed."

Maxine slouched into a chair and Sarah took the big cushion on the floor. "Who knew a ninety minute massage, manicure, pedicure, and facial could just suck the life right out of you?" Sarah said.

"I think I'm going to arrange to have this done monthly," Maxine said.

"Wouldn't you worry your bones would turn to Jell-O?" Robin asked. A rubbery arm covered her eyes, blocking out the track lighting.

"At this point, I don't think I'd care." Maxine closed her eyes. "I'm hungry, but I honestly don't want to move."

Sarah rose on her elbow. "How are you feeling about tomorrow, Robin? We haven't had a lot of time to talk about how you and Tony got back together."

Robin rolled her head and looked at her youngest sister. "I am not as nervous as I was. Tony has been praying with me daily about my fears. I've talked to Sofia and Caroline a couple of times. Somehow, the wedding night thing doesn't horrify me as much as it did."

Maxine shuddered. "I don't think I can ever get married."

With a snort, Sarah stretched. "You fall in and out of love daily, Maxi. How could you ever commit to one man and marriage?"

Only Robin saw the hurt cross Maxine's face before she blithely answered, "Hence my point."

Robin sat up, slowly. "I would have said six months ago that I'd never even date, much less marry. Obviously, God's plans for us aren't always what we have in mind, for which I am infinitely thankful." She groaned and pushed her loose body to her feet. "Rehearsal is at seven, dinner at Barry's immediately after. I have some errands to run. Don't be late."

ROBIN put her hands in the pockets of her trench coat and waited for Peter to unlock the back door of the church. "I'm hoping for warmer weather tomorrow afternoon," she said with a smile.

"Supposed to be lovely tomorrow. With everything else, you should not stress about that," Caroline said, hugging her close. Their five foster kids played a game of chase on the lawn next to the building.

Peter finally got the door unlocked and opened it wide, letting Robin and Caroline precede him. "Lads and lasses," Caroline sing-songed with a clap of her hands, and all five children never broke stride. They just pivoted on their feet and dashed into the open church.

The women slipped inside and Caroline went to a far

wall, throwing switches to light up the room. They crossed the hall, passing administrative offices, and went through the door leading to the main sanctuary through the choir loft. Caroline threw some more switches, and the sanctuary lit up.

"Oh Robin, how beautiful!" she exclaimed. Then, her voice took on a warning note. "Kids, don't touch a thing. Absolutely nothing."

Huge bouquets of white roses, freesia, and lisianthus stood in tall pedestals at the end of the aisle near the main doors, and white cloth draped from the pedestals and swooping from pew to pew, closing off the main aisle. Where the cloth attached to the pew, red and white roses in bouquets held together with white satin ribbon were attached. At the front of the church, identical pillars of flowers flanked the pulpit next to large candelabras.

"Thank you. I think the decorators did a tremendous job," Robin said, turning when the door behind her opened. In walked Maxine and Sarah. "Hi you two," she said with a grin. Nervous excitement fluttered in her chest.

"Hello, bride," Maxine said, hugging Robin. She stepped back and took off her coat. "Do you want me to hang up your coat, too?"

Robin shook her head, "No. I'll leave it on for now."

The door opened again and the photographer, Gerald Parr, came in. "Gerald," she said, walking forward with her hand extended. "Welcome to Boston Bible."

"Thank you," he said as he shook her hand. "This architecture is amazing. I may take some time in the morning and just snap photos of the building."

"Peter here is one of the pastors. I'm sure he could speak for the church and say they didn't mind."

"Absolutely," Peter said.

The door opened again and Tony, Barry, and Derrick came in. Tony went straight to Robin. "*Cara*, my bride to be." He gave her a gentle kiss, then hugged her tight, giving her a reassuring squeeze. "Are you ready?"

With a nervous laugh, she said, "We're still missing a few people."

As if on cue, the Rabonovich's came in followed by Stephanie Giordano. Sofia Rabonovich set down the box she carried and went to Robin, putting her hands on her shoulders, kissing both of her cheeks. "My dear, how incredibly exciting."

Robin nodded and whispered, "No one knows."

Craig came in while Tony and Abram were shaking hands. "I'm not late, am I?"

"Not at all," Tony said, walking to his future father-in-law with his hand extended. "We are so honored that you're giving Robin away."

"I'm thanking God for the chance to be doing things right for once," Craig said, cheeks fusing bright pink with color.

The far door opened, and two high school boys from the youth group came in together. Peter held up a hand in greeting. "Good to see you boys. Thank you for arriving very nearly on time."

The only redhead in the group said, "My mom said to tell you again how much she appreciates you asking us to do this, Mr. V."

Tony smiled. "I'm sure you'll do a great job ushering. There are twenty of you all together, and I know Stephanie has you meeting her for instruction and training in the morning, but you two will be part of the ceremony, so I wanted you to be here tonight."

"And now," Tony said, putting an arm around Robin's

shoulders. "We have a surprise for you all."

Robin's fingers shook slightly, not from nerves but just from general excitement, as she worked the belt loose on her coat. As soon as it was loose, she shrugged out of it, revealing a white satin tea-length dress with short capped sleeves and a scrolling pattern of pearls sewn into the skirt.

Maxine gasped. "Seriously?" she asked, laughing. "I love it!"

"What's going on?" Sarah asked.

"We decided instead of the big hoopla tomorrow, we wanted to experience our most special day with the people closest to us rather than share it with another thousand people," Robin said.

Sarah's eyes narrowed. "What am I not understanding?"

Maxine put her hand on her hip. "They're actually going to get married tonight. This isn't practice—it's for real."

Caroline clapped her hands and threw her head back and laughed. "Fantastic!"

"Wait," Derrick said. "What about tomorrow? Did you cancel everyone coming?"

"Not at all," Tony said. "We'll still go through all the motions. But Robin thought, and I agreed, that she would enjoy the day much more if the added stress of getting married wasn't weighing down on her."

Barry frowned. "Isn't that the point of tomorrow? The stress of getting married?"

Robin walked up to him and slipped her arm around his waist, hugging him to her. "I've been trying to get him to elope with me since he proposed. Don't stop this now, Barry."

He laughed and squeezed her then released her. "I'm

glad you didn't elope. Well, until now. Tony enjoys the hoopla too much."

With a sigh Robin said, "I know. God help me, I know."

Stephanie smiled and said, "She told me about it last week, and I have been absolutely bursting with it. What a fun and clever idea!"

Sophia opened the box she carried in and handed simple bouquets of white roses and fresh greenery to Maxine, Sarah, and Caroline.

"You want me to go ahead and walk you down the aisle now," Craig asked, "or wait for tomorrow?"

"We still need to practice for tomorrow, so we're going to go through all of the motions. But, the ceremony will be real and we'll say our vows," Robin said.

The door opened again and the church's organist and sound manager came in together. They stopped briefly to confer with Abram and Stephanie before she went to the huge pipe organ and flipped switches to get it turned on and the sound manager went back out the door to go up to the sound booth in the balcony.

Abram clapped his hands. "Is everyone ready?"

Robin, her sisters, and Caroline, with Angel Dove and Isaac, all went to the back of the church with Craig while Tony, Barry, Derrick, and Peter went out the side doors at the front of the church. They left the doors propped open so that they could hear Stephanie's directions.

Sarah fiddled with the ribbon on her bouquet. "I wish you'd told us. We could have been prepared."

Robin put an arm around her shoulders. "We intentionally didn't tell anyone but Stephanie, who needed to make flower and dress arrangements for me, and Abram, who will be officiating. We wanted it to be a surprise."

Sarah looked at Maxine. "You didn't know?"

With a shake of her head, Maxine confirmed it. "No. This is a huge surprise for me. I'm thrilled though." She turned to Robin. "What are you guys doing tonight?"

Robin felt her cheeks heat. "We will still have dinner as planned, catered at Barry's house. Only afterward, instead of going back to the hotel, Derrick will take my room and I'll go home with, ah, my husband."

Her upper lip dotted with sweat. Maxine ran a hand over her arm. "You okay with that?"

Robin nodded. "Way more than I would be if it were tomorrow. I can't even handle the thought of dealing with all those eyes and all those people—the small talk and networking—along with the wedding night stress. It was just too much. Tony came up with this idea. I just hope…" She trailed off, not really sure what she meant to say.

Maxine hugged her. "Everything will be magical," she said in Robin's ear. "I believe that."

Robin fanned her face and turned to Craig. "Ready, dad?"

"Kinda glad to be getting a practice in before the real thing, that's for sure," he said, offering his arm. Gerald came down the aisle and snapped a photo just as Robin put her hand on his arm.

From the front of the church, Stephanie held a microphone and tapped it to make sure it was on. "Okay, here's the order of services. Before any of the wedding party come out, there's a soloist. She's going to come and take microphone B and move to here," Stephanie said, walking to the left side of the stage. "She'll sing, and when she finishes, Tony, you, Abram, and your party will come through the doors together and take your places." She paused. "You can come now."

The men came together and Stephanie directed them where to stand. "Okay," she said, "once they're in place, then the two ushers will take the cords on the runner that's back there and walk forward, together pulling it open." The two youth rushed to take the cords and started walking. As the runner opened, Robin could see the beautiful scrolling "V" and the intricate artwork around it. "Come all the way to the front and it should run out just—" the roll ended and they were left holding the cords and an empty holder right in front of Tony and Abram. "Perfect!"

Stephanie continued, "Now the organist will be playing some music the whole time. As soon as they finish the roll, Angel Dove and Isaac will walk together." She looked at Tony but continued to speak into the mike. "Is he still going to carry the rings?"

Tony nodded. "We'll exchange rings again tomorrow. No one need know our practice was the real thing but us."

"So, Angel Dove and Isaac will come down the aisle, followed by the bridal party with Caroline first, then Sarah, and finally Maxi." Stephanie looked at notes as she spoke. Isaac held his sister's hand as they walked with some trepidation, down the long aisle. Eyes wide behind the round glasses, he kept his face focused on his father's, who waited for him at the end.

As soon as they were four rows into the march, Stephanie said, "Okay, now Caroline." She directed Sarah and Maxine at the same time. As they came up front, she told each of them where to stand and how to face the audience. When Maxine was in place, the organist paused for one heart beat, then two, and then played the beginning chords of the wedding march.

Robin looked at Craig. "You ready?"

"As ever," he said, patting her hand that gripped his

other arm. While the familiar music played, Robin and Craig slowly walked down the aisle, and she looked at Tony and smiled. His face was serious, almost intense, but when she smiled, he relaxed and smiled back.

It seemed to take forever to reach the front. She and Craig stopped in front of Tony and Abram.

"Who gives this bride to this groom?" Abram asked.

Craig cleared his throat twice before he spoke, "I do." His voice rang clearly through the church.

Stephanie said, "Craig, at this point, you'll raise her veil."

Craig mocked raising her veil. He looked so uncomfortable, that Robin hugged him. Blinking back tears, she stepped forward and took Tony's hand. Holding her hand, he turned and faced Abram.

In a strong and rich voice, Abram said, "It really is a joy to be here tonight, gathered with you, Tony and Robin, and surrounded here by friends. It is such a privilege to officiate this celebration. You two are very special to my Sofia and me, and I thank you for inviting me to be a part of it."

Robin thought about the first time she met Abram. While she and Tony had sat in the Rabonovich's home and had after-church cake and coffee, he had very kindly and lovingly instructed her on how to start reading her Bible.

"After the ceremony today, I will sign the marriage certificate. Everyone who has been married in recent years has a piece of paper that certifies that they had a wedding. Some folks have it in a nice frame, up on the wall somewhere in their house. Some might have it in a lock box with other important documents in order to keep it safe. Regardless of what you do with this piece of paper, I want to tell something I hope you never forget—it's just a piece of paper. Really. That's all. A piece of paper is not a marriage. In fact, everything we are doing today is not a marriage."

Robin looked at Tony. He must have felt her glance, because he shifted his eyes from Abram and looked over at her. They had conspired to get married tonight instead of tomorrow so that this moment, this ceremony, could be something just them and the people closest to them could share. She grinned a secret grin meant for Tony alone. Despite nearly bursting with the desire to share the plan with her sisters, she didn't spoil the surprise. That made this all the more fun, she thought.

"Don't get me wrong, this is a great day—a beautiful day. It is wonderful to be here in this place, with all these friends, witnessing your vows to one another in this historic building where thousands of others through four generations have said their own vows. But as good as it is to be here, we should all remember that this is a wedding, not a marriage. What makes a marriage is what comes next."

It was hard not to lean over and kiss Tony. He had looked so intense, his dark eyes so serious. But when she gave him that secret grin, everything about him softened and he smiled and winked at her.

"What makes a marriage is what you do tomorrow, and the next day, and the following weeks and months and years and decades to come… growing older and weaker in the flesh and wiser and stronger in love. There is a verse of scripture that claims, 'No one has greater love than this, to lay down one's life for one's friends.' Chances are that you will never be asked to give up your life for your spouse. But, you will have to give up yourself for your spouse every day from now on. Marriage is not a piece of paper."

Since Abram was speaking directly to them, Robin looked back at their friend. She thought forward to the coming night and realized that anticipation had replaced the trepidation. Excitement had replaced the fear. Once she acknowledged what had eaten at her for weeks, once she knew where all of her hesitation in marrying Tony lay, it gave her a target, a focus, and she started fighting it back.

"Marriage is a gift. Marriage is a choice. Marriage is sacrifice. And marriage is when two become one. Robin, today you will give yourself entirely to Tony. And Tony, today you will give yourself entirely to Robin. In a moment, those are exactly the words that we will use to begin this ceremony: Tony, will you give yourself to Robin? Robin, will you give yourself to Tony?

"Marriage is a gift, the gift of yourself, your heart, your thoughts, and your hopes and dreams… Marriage is the gift of your life. And it is not just today."

It amazed Robin that what she had discovered through Tony's willingness to sacrifice his entire life in order to be with her, that he needed her as much as she needed him. How had she missed that in this courtship? He seemed so strong, confident, and so self assured that she didn't think he needed anyone. She never truly understood the depths of his feelings for her.

"Every day from here forward, you must continue to give yourselves to one another. Today you will state a public vow and commit yourselves to each other. Every morning after this one, you will have to wake up and choose to recommit yourselves to each other. Marriage is a choice. Marriage means letting go of petty fights about who's right and wrong. It means putting your spouse's interests, wants and desires, and happiness ahead of your own. It means, Tony, that after today Robin's happiness is more important than yours. And it means, Robin, that after today Tony's happiness is more important than yours."

Out of the corner of her eye, she saw Tony's head turn, so she looked at him. At Abram's words about his happiness, Tony raised an eyebrow and with a teasing glint in his eye, he winked at her. Robin had to swallow a laugh.

"Marriage is sacrificing for each other and acting as one. That is what it means to become one flesh, forever joined together… Cleaved unto each other. You are each your wedding gift to one another. Your wedding day is the symbol of your marriage to each other. And your marriage is the gift of continuing to give the gift of yourselves to each other. And with that gift to each other, with that shared love, I know that you will have a marriage that will last through the ages, and stand as a witness to all of the love of God. God bless you."

They both looked back at Abram, who looked each one of them in the eye and smiled at them. "But that is enough of me because today is about the two of you. Tony and Robin, I invite you to come and begin the adventure of your marriage by declaring your vows to one another here in this place."

He gestured with his hands, telling Tony and Robin to turn and face each other. Stephanie said, "Robin, at this point, hand your bouquet to Maxine. Maxine, be prepared, because her bouquet is heavy, so you might want to prep and hand yours to Sarah."

The bouquet that Robin held tonight was very small and very simple. She handed it to Maxine and turned back to Tony, letting him take both of her hands. She looked into the eyes of the man with whom she was about to vow to become one, and felt excitement, peace, love. Gone was apprehension, gone was fear. She whispered a "thank you" to God for answering her prayers.

Abram smiled and nodded. "I am going to pray. Please bow your heads." As everyone complied, he spoke into the silent, reverent room. "Jehovah God, we thank You for the way that You work in our lives. We know You brought Tony and Robin together with a purpose, and I am praying that You bless this union, strengthen their bond, and let them work for You in a powerful way in your ministry. Guide their future, convict their hearts, and touch the lives of their future children. We are so honored to be in front of You today, and we thank You for giving us this opportunity. Amen."

Abram looked at Stephanie. "It is my understanding that they have their own vows?"

"We worked on them together. Here they are," Tony said pulling a piece of paper out of his jacket pocket.

"Okay," Abram said, waving a hand toward them. "This is where you say your vows. Let me see." He cleared his throat and started reading.

CHAPTER SIXTEEN

Robin and Tony held hands as they walked up the walk to Barry's home. Just as they reached the door, Barry threw it open. "I thought you might have gotten lost," he joked.

"The photographer wanted a few more shots of us before we left," Robin said. She gestured behind her. "I hope you don't mind that he's here, too."

"Of course not," Barry said, stepping aside so they could come in. "The more the merrier."

As they entered the large front room, Jacqueline came toward them wearing a tight black dress and three-inch red heels. "Antonio, Robin, darlings, you're here." She air kissed both of their cheeks and stepped back, leaving a cloying smell of perfume behind her. "The caterers had to hold dinner from being served waiting on you."

The tone of disapproval did little to damper Robin's spirits. "We missed you at the rehearsal," Robin said. She slipped off her coat and Jacqueline's eyebrow rose.

"I had to handle the caterers," she said distracted as she

looked Robin's dress up and down. Her face became frozen solid as she pointedly looked at their left hands and noted the band of diamonds on Robin's and the large gold band on Tony's. "Apparently, I missed something."

Tony comfortably slipped his arm over Robin's shoulders. "We surprised everyone and had the official wedding ceremony tonight," he said. "It's too bad you couldn't delegate the dinner and join us."

"Someone should have mentioned it," Jacqueline said through gritted teeth. She turned her head and looked at her husband.

"He was just as surprised as everyone else, Jacqui. Sheathe your claws," Tony said in a warning. "You will not make a scene or you will not be welcome tomorrow, and we both know you will be looking just stunning for as many publicity shots as possible tomorrow."

Jacqueline stepped backward and took a deep breath, then lifted one of her red curls before she patted her hair to make sure everything stayed smooth. "No worries, Antonio. No scenes. Don't be ridiculous." She looked at Robin from head to toe. "Cute dress. Very retro. Nice choice."

Robin smoothed the skirt. "Thank you." Needing to not be at odds with her husband's best friend, she stepped forward and linked her arm with Jacqueline's, steering her away from Tony. "I had a great time shopping with you last week. This is all very new to me, and I learned so much from you. Can we make plans again soon?"

"Of course, darling," Jacqueline said, shooting Tony a parting glance. "When you get back from your honeymoon, we'll need to get your summer wardrobe built. We'll make plans to go."

"I'd like that very much, thank you." Having

successfully steered her away from Tony, Robin disengaged her arm. "And thank you again for hosting the dinner tonight. I know the groom's family is supposed to be the host for the rehearsal dinner."

"Well, Antonio has always considered my husband as a brother, for whatever reason." She gestured toward one of the O'Farrell kids. "I need to go rescue my Italian leather furniture from those... children," she said the last word like it stuck in her mouth.

Robin looked as one of the older O'Farrell's sat down on the white leather sofa and brought his knees up, resting his boots on the seat of the couch. Caroline and Jacqueline both made a beeline for him at the same time.

"Nice place," Maxine said, coming up to Robin and handing her a glass of water. She gestured at the sweeping stairway that led to the rooms upstairs. An open balcony showed several closed doors. "I like the open second floor."

"It makes the room feel huge," Robin said. "Jacqui told me about some photo shoot that some home magazine is coming to do at Tony's apartment. This world is so different from anything we've known."

"You'll fit in. You served most of these people at Benedict's over the years. You know how they think, act, interact. And, you can remember names. That's a huge deal."

Robin nodded and took a long pull of her water. She didn't realize how thirsty she was until she started drinking. "It's less and less intimidating as the days go by."

She felt Tony's hand on her waist and turned her head to smile at him. "You handled that with expertise," he said, referring to Jacqueline.

"Well, all those years as a waitress and bartender have

taught me the fine art of soothing angry souls," Robin said with a smile.

"Color me impressed. She is often difficult to get along with."

"Nah," Robin said, shaking her head. "She is afraid of not being accepted, so she goes overboard to make sure she is. I feel kind of bad for her."

Tony brought her hand up to his lips and kissed it. "I love your heart," he said.

"And I love you."

"I wasn't finished." Tony said, "I love your heart but please don't fall for Jacqui's tricks. Trust me when I tell you she is not someone anyone needs to feel sorry for. In fact, she is a hungry lion roaming the earth seeking whom she may devour. She has teeth and claws and very often malevolent intent. Know that going into any conversation and guard your heart my beloved bride."

"Tony, you aren't really describing the woman I spent an entire day shopping with."

Tony nodded. "I understand that."

"I guess I'm just surprised to hear you say these things. I mean, look at this party she's hosting."

Tony grinned. "You are so generous with your love, my darling. Listen, Barry is hosting this party. And believe me when I tell you that Jacqui has given him no end of grief over it among many other things. Do me a favor and just watch her when she is around Barry tonight. I trust your instincts and so should you."

Something about Maxine's stance and demeanor changed as Tony spoke. When he concluded his last request, Maxine interrupted. "Hey, I'm starving. Let's make sure they know everyone is here so they can start serving."

ROBIN stood in the middle of the living room and held her hands out, whirling in a circle. She laughed, and the sound filled and satisfied Tony's soul. He smiled, delighting in her.

"We are married," she said with a grin, kicking her shoes off.

"Till death," Tony smiled walking toward her until he could hook her waist with his arm. "Or until I get tired of you," he said.

With a snort, Robin grabbed his tie. "You won't get rid of me that easy."

"I certainly hope not," he said, putting a hand on her cheek. "You are amazing and beautiful. I think what we did tonight was a great idea. Now you can enjoy tomorrow without the added stress of getting married."

Robin slipped her arms around his neck. "I love you, Antonio Viscolli. I am eternally grateful for the day God placed you in my life."

"And I you, *mia moglie*." He smiled and looked into her sapphire blue eyes. "I like that, calling you 'my wife'. I look forward to doing that for many years." He brought his lips down to hers, feeling his breath sweep away at the mere brush of her skin on his. The blood roared in his ears as he deepened the kiss, and he fought for control even as he pulled her tighter to him.

He kissed her and kissed her, drinking her in. Ripping his mouth away, he ran his lips along her jaw to the nape of her neck, inhaling the scent of her perfume, feeling all cognitive thinking sweep away. He felt Robin's hands slide up his head and grip his hair as he kissed the sensitive skin under her ear. Her gasp, the clutch of her hands, the way her body moved against his almost made him lose control, but he clawed for it and grasped it back.

He ripped his head up and tried to take a breath that wasn't consumed with her taste or smell. She placed her lips on his neck, almost mimicking his kiss. "Wait," he panted. His skin burned under her touch.

"Wait for what?" Robin purred, kissing his jaw, placing her lips at the corner of his mouth.

"You need—"

Robin silenced him with her kiss, wrapping her arms around his neck and standing on tiptoe as if she wanted to devour him. When she finally broke her mouth away, she said, "I need you." Framing his face with her hands, she stared into his eyes and he started to drown. "I need you, *mio marito.*"

Hearing her call him her husband in his native tongue broke the last thread of control he clumsily held. Sweeping her into his arms he cradled her to him as he kissed her and carried her into his—into their—bedroom.

CHAPTER SEVENTEEN

Robin opened her eyes, momentarily panicked by the unfamiliar surroundings. Then memories of the night before came flooding back and she slowly sat up, pulling the sheet up with her. She surveyed the room around her with interest, recognizing her bath robe hanging on the back of the open closet door next to his. Boxes lay stacked in a corner labeled "bedroom," obviously waiting for her to fully move in.

She sat up against a mahogany headboard. A heavy cream-colored cover trimmed in brown lay folded at the foot of the bed. A huge Oriental rug covered the floor. Against one wall, a fireplace had wood stacked next to it ready to be lit. In front of it two leather chairs flanked a large chess set. On the walls hung paintings of Boston, various locations at various times of the year.

Tony came into the room wearing khaki pants and a white shirt open at the neck. He carried a steaming mug of coffee. Her heart immediately started racing at the sight of him. She wondered if seeing him in the morning would do that for the rest of her life.

"Good morning, *cara*," he said. He set the mug on the night stand next to the bed and sat on the edge of the bed by her hip. Putting a hand on either side of her, he leaned forward and brushed her lips with his own. She sighed and tried to deepen the kiss, but he chuckled and pulled back. "As much as spending the day with you in bed really appeals to me, we're running late as it is. Much to do today," he said. "We have to get married, after all."

He presented her with the coffee and she took the first heavenly sip. As the caffeine worked its way through her body, she pulled her knees up and wrapped her free arm around her legs. "We're already married. Can't we just skip to the cake?"

Tony laughed. "Cake will come soon enough." He kissed her again and stood. "And then the honeymoon." He wiggled his eyebrows. "Which means all day in bed if we want."

Robin grinned and put her arms over her head, stretching. When the sheet fell, she watched Tony's eyes darken. "Oh, I want," she said giggling. She pulled the sheet back up. "Where are my clothes?"

Tony cleared his throat and sweat popped out on his forehead. He took a step backward and gestured at the closet. "There's new and old in there. The clothes you purchased with Jacqui are all put away. If I were you, I'd wear something from there. Our friends in the press are going to be everywhere today."

"Press?"

He shrugged. "You'll be fine." He smiled and bent to kiss her one more time. "Get dressed before I make us late to our own wedding." He started from the room, but paused and snapped his fingers. "I have a car arriving in thirty minutes to take you to the hotel. Your sisters and Caroline are already there. I have to run."

"Where will you be?" Robin asked.

"The groom isn't supposed to see the bride before the wedding, remember? The next time I see you, you'll be walking down the aisle toward me."

SARAH stepped into the massive Grand Ballroom of the Viscolli hotel. The sight that greeted her nearly took her breath away. Hundreds of tables covered in ivory and gold, formally set with gold-rimmed china and crystal filled the room. Each table had a beautiful centerpiece of a round ball of ivory roses sitting on a tall pillar. The chairs at the tables were covered with ivory brocade and tied at the top of the chair with a large red ribbon that formed a bow on the back of the chair.

At the far end of the room, massive doors opened to the tent area, but the carpet and ceiling matched so well that Sarah could barely tell where the ballroom ended and the tent began. Waiters and bus boys worked inside the tent, covering chairs, setting tables, and placing centerpieces.

The long head table spanned the front of the room with a gorgeous red and ivory rose centerpiece that ran along its entire length. The chairs for Tony and Robin, at the middle of the table, looked like thrones fit for a king and queen. And, honestly, as far as Sarah could tell, Tony seemed like royalty. This wedding certainly felt like the royal wedding, Sarah thought, especially with the mob of reporters camped outside the hotel and roving the hotel lobby. She imagined the church would be just as chaotic.

Sarah really liked Tony. Having been raised in the church and taught to work and give to God, she loved that he dedicated his entire life and fortune to ministry. She knew he would do anything for anyone if he could. He had certainly proven it by opening his home to Derrick.

Thinking of that boy set her teeth on edge. Tony met him outside of a seedy bar in the very worst neighborhood possible, and a month later the boy was living with him? She wouldn't care, it would be just fine, except that Robin and Sarah were going to be living there, too.

Not wanting thoughts of him to ruin this day, because certainly his presence during the ceremony would be enough, Sarah shook her head and walked over to the far end of the ballroom, away from the open doors and the tent area, to where the cake table was set up.

The massive, amazing structure was simply stunning. Eight tiers rose up in ivory colored buttercream. Beautifully hand crafted sugar flowers of roses, lilies, hydrangea, ranunculus, and orchids created an amazing waterfall of flowers spilling from the top on down the tiers, widening as it reached the huge bottom tier.

Sarah shifted her overnight bag on her shoulder and turned, looking at the room from this angle. Robin had absolutely outdone herself. Well, Robin with the help and guidance of Stephanie and Maxine. Without them, Robin had joked that they'd have had a backyard wedding in blue jeans with chocolate cake.

Sarah thought back to the first time she met Robin. She had no memory of her life before waking up in her then foster parents' home. In an effort to protect and shield her, they'd made no mention of sisters or a murdered mother or the life from which she'd come to them. They just told her that God gave her to them, and shushed any possible questions until she just learned not to ask them.

But on the morning of her fifteenth birthday, Robin and Maxine sat at the kitchen table at her parents' house, not knowing she didn't know them. Robin had been fighting in the court system for visitation rights, and finally won the right to visit Sarah for an hour each week. Sarah fell in love with her sisters, though they intimidated her. They were hard, with hard eyes and air of desperation about them that Sarah thought needed to be avoided. But she waited all week for the time to arrive when she could see them again, and gradually got to know them.

When her high school graduation loomed in front of her, her parents broke the news - they would not be able to afford college on any level. Because they did not believe in borrowing money, and because Sarah had been taught at a very young age not to borrow money, the idea of a student loan repelled her. Struggling to find a way to afford to go to college, Robin's suggestion that she pay for it was a welcome option. The only condition was that Sarah live with her and Maxine while she went to school. Sarah was thrilled. Not only would she get to actually go to school, but she would get to know these beautiful and brilliant sisters of hers.

Her parents had objected, but they relented knowing that it was the only way Sarah could go.

She didn't fit in with the two of them. She ate differently - from her earliest memory, the smell and taste of meat made her physically ill, so she ate a completely vegan diet - no meat and no meat products. And, she had dedicated her life to Christ. Robin and Maxine, though they intellectually knew that about her, didn't understand it so therefore didn't bring it up. Growing up in a Christian home with a loving family left her with absolutely nothing in common with her sisters.

For two years, she watched Robin work herself into the ground. The first year was the hardest, because Sarah and Maxine were both in school at the same time. At just 24 years of age, Robin worked two jobs six-days-a-week to pay for tuition and books for both sisters. Maxine constantly tried to get a job to help out, and Sarah offered as well, but Robin adamantly insisted that she be the one to do this for them.

After Tony came into her life, Sarah saw her sister gradually relax. The desperation on her face slid away and became peace. She watched Robin give her life to Christ, and sat in Tony's big downtown church to see her oldest sister baptized.

As soon as Robin became saved, Sarah felt like they had something in common, and suddenly, they started talking—full blown conversations that Sarah actually enjoyed. It was such a relief to actually feel a part of Robin's life instead of another burden on her shoulders, and a part of her that she constantly held back softened and she grew to love both of her sisters like she didn't even know was possible.

And now, Tony was giving Robin a royal wedding. Sarah knew, because she knew Tony, that a desire to show Robin how much he valued her motivated him—which was why he never gave in to Robin wanting to elope. He wanted this pomp and circumstance so that he could show Robin off to the watching world. Sarah believed, with all of her heart, that there wasn't another person on earth who deserved this kind of pampering more than Robin.

She put her hands to her mouth and blinked back tears of joy at the beauty and style that the day would bring. Excited, honored to be a part of it, she said a quick prayer of thanksgiving to God for giving Robin the steadfastness to battle her parents for visitation, or Sarah might have gone her whole life never meeting her two wonderful sisters.

Her phone buzzed in her pocket, breaking her reverie. She pulled it out and scanned the text from Maxine, asking her location. "BALLROOM" she wrote back, and slipped the phone back into her pocket.

By the time she crossed the room, Maxine entered wearing dark sunglasses, black yoga pants, and a tight-fitting fleece. "Holy cow, it's like a zoo out there. Did you see the news vans?"

"I did. It's hysterical. How do you look so fashionable dressed like that?" Sarah asked. "I don't think I'll look that good in our dresses tonight."

Maxine slipped off her glasses and hugged her sister. "Don't be silly. You are gorgeous." She spun in a circle. "Look at this place! Amazing!"

"I know. You and Stephanie really helped Robin. I am stunned."

"We actually just guided her in the beginning. Once she got her feet wet, I was able to pull back a bit. She just didn't know she could do it until she did it." Maxine put her hand into the pocket of her fleece and pulled out a keycard. "Suite 1914. It has a couple of bedrooms, a full living room and dining room, and a fully stocked kitchen. Should be perfect for our little hair and makeup party today."

Sarah looked at her watch. "What time will everyone be here?"

"Caroline is bringing Angel Dove with her at ten. The stylist and her assistants will be here at nine, but we need to get Robin's hair rolled before they do anything else. I have makeup coming at one."

"What about Robin?"

They left the ballroom. "Tony texted me twenty minutes ago and said she'd be here by nine."

"We have time to grab breakfast then," Sarah said, putting an arm around Maxine's waist.

"Already ordered, sister of mine. Hopefully, room service will beat us to our room."

ROBIN sat back in the chair, eyes closed, while one woman coated color on her eyelid and another pinned yet even more baby's breath into the intricate structure of curls and twists of her hair. She could hear Caroline's lyrical voice as she read a book to Angel Dove and smiled at the sound.

"Open," the makeup artist said. Robin opened her eyes and the woman took her chin, tilting her head this way and that before nodding and stepping back. "All done. I know it feels like a lot, but when you see pictures, you'll be pleased."

"Thank you," Robin said.

The hair stylist stepped away as well. "Ready for the veil," she said.

"Go on into the bedroom and get your dress on," Caroline said. "Maxine? Go help her."

Robin's head felt heavy with the weight of the pins and flowers. She wanted to put her hand up and feel and fuss, but as many hours as she sat while they worked it into place, she was afraid to mess it up.

Maxine followed her into the bedroom. She already had on her dress - a strapless red gown that shimmered when she moved. It fell just below her knees in the front and dropped nearly to the floor in the back. She wore red heels the color of the dress. It looked stunning on all three of the bridesmaids, which was a feat considering the differences in age and body style. Maxine's hair was twisted into an intricate knot on the base of her skull, with tendrils of hair left flowing down along her temples.

Robin unbuttoned her blouse and slipped out of it, then slipped off her sweat pants. She already had on her white silk stockings.

Maxine carefully pulled her dress off of the hanger and unsnapped, unzipped, and unhooked it to allow Robin to step into it, then she slid it up and zipped, snapped, and hooked it into place.

"Wow," Maxine said, stepping back. "That looks even a million times more fabulous than it did when you tried it on without the makeup and the hair.

A wide full-length mirror had been installed in the room for her and she walked to it. When she saw her reflection, she was speechless. She wore heart-shaped ruby earrings that Caroline had loaned her. "A Valentine's Day gift from last year," she'd said. "A treasure of mine." On her wrist, she wore the antique gold bracelets that Maxine and Sarah had given her as a wedding present. On her neck, she wore the new ruby and diamond necklace Tony gave her, and on her finger, she wore the blue sapphire engagement ring.

Maxine held up a mirror so she could see the back of her hair. A wide, flat braid started at the crown of her head and snaked around and formed into a bun. The stylist had pulled the strands of the braid and pinned them back so that the bun looked like an open rose. Baby's breath was dotted all through the braid.

"Wow," Robin said. As much as the makeup artist had worked on her face, Robin had felt certain she'd end up looking like a clown. Instead, the makeup, while heavy, looked so subtle and exceptionally worked with Robin's face. "I look like a princess," she whispered.

Sarah came in and stopped short. "Robin," she said on a breath, "wow."

Maxine laughed. "I know! It's here. It's finally here."

Sarah clapped her hands. "I can't believe it's finally time. Are you nervous?"

Robin shook her head. "Strangely, no. I think what we did yesterday took away all the nerves. I'm just ready for cake."

Sarah laughed. "Now shoes!" She went to the bed and grabbed the small shoebox. It contained a pair of simple white heels with a sparkling red ribbon woven through the top of them to a bow on the back. Robin lifted the skirt of her dress and slipped them on.

"Gerald!" Maxine said. The door immediately opened and Gerald came in with two cameras with different lenses hanging by straps around his neck. "We're ready for the veil."

Robin carefully perched on a sitting stool while Maxine and Sarah pinned the veil onto her head and Gerald took a dozen pictures. When they were finished, all three women were crying and hugged each other tightly in a group hug.

CHAPTER EIGHTEEN

Robin followed the security guard through the hotel lobby. She wanted to duck and hide from the whirring sounds of cameras, but she didn't. She held her shoulders back and walked next to her sisters through the crowd and into the waiting limo.

They all piled in... Robin, Maxine, Sarah, Caroline, and Angel Dove. Gerald sat in front with the driver.

"Well, that was sure a circus," Caroline said. She put a hand to her temple. Somehow, the hairstylist had managed to contain her wild red hair and keep it contained. Robin had never seen her look so beautiful before.

"Tony called and said it was worse at the church."

"Is everyone there?" Caroline asked.

"He said the guys all got there about two."

Sarah brushed at the skirt of her dress. "Oh to be a man at times like this."

"But then you wouldn't look as pretty," Angel Dove said, pushing away from Caroline and climbing into Sarah's lap. She wore a dress with a white sleeveless top made out of shiny satin and a pattern of red heart-shaped crystals sewn into the neckline. The skirt was long and shiny red satin trimmed in white. On her feet, she wore white socks with red hearts and white patent leather shoes. A crown of baby red roses and white baby's breath would go on her head before she walked down the aisle.

"And I wouldn't have had the chance to spend the day with you," Sarah said, putting her cheek on the top of Angel Dove's head.

Robin felt the burn of tears watching Sarah warm to her friends. She looked at Caroline and smiled. "I can't wait to see if Isaac actually put the tux on."

"He better, and he knows it."

"He also knows you're all bluster."

Caroline laughed as the limo slowed and came to a stop. "True."

"Wow," Maxine said, looking out the window. "This is outrageous."

A security team kept the crowds behind a barricade. As soon as the driver had the door open, Robin could hear the noise of the crowd. It drowned out every sound around them. Her stomach dropped at the sight of everyone yelling and taking pictures and she felt nerves dance up into her chest. She wanted to duck her head and run inside, but instead she waved at the crowd then stepped back and waited for everyone to get out of the car.

They walked calmly together through the double doors of the church, which shut behind them, cutting off the noise.

"What in the world?" Caroline said.

"Tony's guest list brought the crowds," Barry said approaching them. "Celebrities, politicians, religious leaders… I'm glad he thought ahead to security."

"There you are," Stephanie said, rushing toward them. She wore a stunning rose colored suit that went well with her silver hair. Her heels clicked rapidly on the tile floor. "Oh Robin, girls, you all look amazing."

Robin put a hand over her necklace. She could feel the furious pounding of her heart. "I'm suddenly very nervous."

"I'm sure. Me too!" She gestured toward the sanctuary. "Let's get some pictures made before your guests arrive. We have an hour tops."

For the next forty-five minutes, Robin sat, stood, and posed for more pictures than she could possibly count. Alone, with bridesmaids, with sisters, with Abram, with groomsmen, she smiled and smiled and smiled until her face hurt. Then she drank some water and smiled some more.

Her makeup artist came at one point and refreshed lipstick and powdered her nose, and then she sat for a dozen more poses.

"Enough," she said, holding up her hand. "We have enough pictures."

Stephanie looked at her watch. "That's good, because we need to go ahead and sequester you, anyway."

She followed Stephanie through the church and into a small room off of the narthex. Through the door, she could hear the noise of the crowds every time the main doors opened and closed, and could hear the conversations of the ushers and guests in the lobby.

She sat on a small stool and waited. "This is where it's hard," she said. "Staying hidden instead of just getting it over with."

"There are a lot of people to seat," Sarah said. "I'm surprised you went with youth boys for ushers. I'm sure you could have hired trained staff."

"If you expect big things out of youth, they'll do big things," Robin said. "So says Tony, anyway."

Maxine came closer and spoke softly. "You okay. I mean, about, uh, last night?"

Robin felt the heat on her cheeks but took Maxine's hand. "Oh yes. Unimaginably okay."

Maxine squeezed her hand. "Good. What a relief. When you didn't say anything all day, I worried."

Robin cleared her throat. "It's not exactly a conversation starter."

Sarah laughed. "No doubt."

Robin felt her whole face flush and fanned herself with her hands. "Girls!"

Stephanie came in by a back door. "Your dad is outside. Can he come in?"

Robin stood. "Of course."

Stephanie stuck her head out the door and then opened it wide enough to allow Craig to come in. He crossed the room and stood in front of her, tugging on his collar. He looked great in his black tuxedo, white shirt, and black bow tie. "Some lady in a pink dress said to come in here and get a flower."

Maxine went to the boxes of flowers on a far table and found the white rose boutonniere that had a tag on it with Craig's name. She walked back toward them and handed it to Robin to pin on him. "You look so nice, dad," Robin said. "You clean up good."

He stepped back and raised his hand in her direction. "Look who's talking. You look like a princess. Hard to believe that you are mine."

"I think it just goes to show you that any of us can clean up good if we want." In a spontaneous motion, she kissed his cheek. "I'm so proud of you and so happy you've come to know the Lord. Thank you for agreeing to give me away."

With a large hand, he clumsily patted her shoulder and swallowed tears. "You do an old man proud," he whispered, then pivoted and exited the room. Robin smiled at his retreating back, and said a silent prayer of thanks to God for this time she's had with Craig. She worried a little that he would be put back in prison by the time she got home from her honeymoon.

"That was incredibly sweet," Sarah said. "There's nothing like a dad. I'm so thankful that mine has always been such a good friend to me."

"You're very lucky," Maxine said, her mouth in a thin line. Someone rapped sharply on the door. After a few heartbeats, Barry stuck his head inside.

"We're getting ready to get into our positions," he said. He looked around the room and gave a low whistle. "You ladies all look absolutely beautiful."

"Thank you, Barry," Robin said, walking up to him. He came further into the room and she brushed at the jacket on his shoulder. "Can you find Stephanie? I still seem to have boutonnieres for the guys."

As she spoke, Stephanie rushed in. "Boutonnieres," she said. "How could I have forgotten?"

"They're right there," Maxine said with a laugh. Stephanie grabbed the long flat box and rushed out of the room with it. Maxine looked at Barry. "Guess you should follow her."

He smiled. "Guess I should. See you guys at the end of the aisle!"

He shut the door behind him. Robin felt her whole body start quaking. She put a hand on her chest and sat back on the stool. "I—don't—know—I—can—do—this." She felt like she couldn't take a deep enough breath.

Caroline rushed over and put her hands on Robin's bare shoulders. "Just breathe, lass. Nice and easy. Slowly in and slowly out."

Robin's vision started to gray. "Can I have some water?" she whispered.

Sarah rushed to hand her a bottle of water.

"Thank you." Robin took a sip of the water, then tilted it back and drained the whole bottle. She gently patted her mouth, worried about messing up lipstick if she wiped against it. "That's better."

Maxine knelt next to her chair. "You got this," she said. "The part in front of the crowd will be over in no time."

"Then the best part starts," Sarah said.

Robin closed her eyes and concentrated on Tony's face, thought about worshipping with him in the sanctuary at this very church and felt calmer. They were just people—a thousand people—but just people.

She stood, feeling better. As she stood, she heard the sound of Nat King Cole's "When I Fall in Love" and the sweet melodious voice of a friend from church start singing the song.

"I think that's our cue, friends." She brushed at her skirt. "Caroline, can you distribute our bouquets?"

"First," Caroline said, "we are going to pray." She held out her hands, and Maxine, Sarah, Angel Dove, and Robin all joined hands, forming a circle. "Dear God, I pray you give Robin a calming strength to get through the next few hours. Give her physical strength, ease her pain in those shoes, and let her just enjoy herself and all of the hard work she put into it."

Robin hugged her when she finished praying. "Thank

you, my friend. You are a blessing to me."

"Likewise, love."

Stephanie came rushing in. "This is it," she said, all grins. "I can't wait to see their faces when they see how beautiful you are, Robin." She went to the table with the bouquets. She handed each of the bridesmaids their bouquets of white roses, and then handed Robin the long flowing bouquet of red and white roses.

"Wow," Robin said, lifting it up and down. "You weren't kidding about the weight."

"Okay, Angel Dove. Let's go find your brother." At Caroline's nod, Angel Dove took Stephanie's hand.

They walked out. Caroline followed in her turn, then Sarah, and Maxine. In the lobby of the church, ten of the twenty ushers milled around, looking smart in their black tuxes. Robin hugged the closest one. "Was it hard organizing everyone?"

"You have a packed house, Robin. I don't think I've ever seen the church this full. We had to have people shift and move to get everyone seats." He tugged at his jacket. "I met Senator Carson. He was really nice. My dad always likes him."

Robin grinned. "That's so exciting."

She heard the last notes of the song play. Everyone lined up at the door, and Craig came to stand by her. Stephanie unhooked her train from the hook on her waist and spread it out behind her while she whispered directions to the two teens tasked with rolling out the runner. The crowd murmured in anticipation during the silence of this act. As the organist began to play, Angel Dove and Isaac, in his tuxedo, entered through the double doors. Robin watched Caroline's head as she kept time with their steps and the organist's rhythm. When it was time, she put her shoulders back, smiled, and stepped into the church.

Sarah looked over her shoulder at Robin. "Yay," she silently cheered. When it was time for her to go, she walked forward.

Maxine grinned and winked at Robin. "You're gorgeous," she said, "Tony's going to fall over." She looked forward, smiled, and started walking.

Robin wanted to go to the doors and peek in, but Stephanie had told her not to because everyone would be craning trying to look at her. Instead, she pulled her veil down and she and Craig waited for Stephanie's signal. When she gestured with her hands, they walked and stood at the entrance.

Robin could see Tony down at the front of the church. The aisle seemed so much longer than it had the night before. When the organist began the wedding march, all of the audience stood to their feet and Robin and Craig started walking down the white runner.

She smiled and made eye contact with friends, church friends, and business friends. When she got closer to the front, she looked right at Tony, and the look of awe and wonder on his face made her realize that every single step in this four-month process had been worth it.

After what seemed like a mile, they reached the end of the aisle. Abram stood in full vestments, looking very handsome and regal. He gestured with his hands and the audience sat down. It took several seconds for everyone to sit and get settled and get quiet.

"Who gives this bride to be married?" he asked.

Craig said in a loud and confident voice, "I do."

Abram nodded, and Craig turned and lifted Robin's veil, smoothly guiding it over her head. Robin held her bouquet with one hand and hugged Craig's neck tight with the other. He cleared his throat and blinked overly wet eyes as he placed Robin's hand in Tony's. As they turned to face Abram, and listened to him talk in beautiful ways about what it meant to be married, Robin whispered to Tony, "I can't believe how much longer that aisle is today than yesterday."

He gave her hand a gentle squeeze. "I didn't think you'd ever make it to me."

She smiled and looked at him. "You look very nice in your Zoot suit."

"Yeah? If you knew how amazing you looked, you'd just be sitting in front of a mirror all day." He lifted her hand and kissed it. "You are the most beautiful woman I have ever laid eyes on."

Robin's heart fluttered at his words. "It was hard to see through this veil."

"I bet."

Abram said, "But that's enough of me because today is about the two of you. Tony and Robin, I invite you to come and begin the adventure of your marriage by declaring your vows to one another here in this place."

She turned and handed Maxine her bouquet. Then she fully faced her husband, placing both of her hands in his. The look in his eyes took her breath away.

"Let everyone hear these words. Tony has proposed matrimony and Robin has graciously accepted. Should there be anyone here who has an objection to the marriage of these two, let that person speak now or forevermore be silent."

Abram waited just a small heartbeat in the silence before continuing. "In the absence of an objection, we will now proceed. Please bow your heads and pray with me."

She bowed her head and listened to the prayer Abram

prayed over their future, their lives, and their ministries. While he spoke, Robin prayed that God would bless them and use them in mighty ways, that He would give them wisdom and strength to face adversaries and attacks. And, at the end, she prayed, for the thousandth time, a prayer of thanksgiving for giving her Tony.

As the congregation said, "Amen," in chorus with Abram, they raised their heads and he looked at Robin. "Will you, Robin, take this man, Tony, to be your beloved bridegroom? Will you respect and honor him, comfort and keep him, in good times and in bad, in times of failure and in times of triumph, for better or for worse, for richer, for poorer, in sickness and in health, and—forsaking all others—remain true and faithful to him for as long as you both shall live?"

Robin smiled. "I will."

Abram nodded. "Then in the presence of God and all those gathered here, repeat this solemn vow which you will uphold from this day forward. I, Robin, promise you, Tony, that I will give you my heart and my life."

Robin repeated the words with a strong and clear voice, making sure she conveyed just how much she meant them.

"I will stand by your side in sorrow or in joy."

"I will comfort and encourage you."

"I will support you in all that you do."

"I will laugh with you and cry with you."

"Above all, I will honor and respect you as your loving wife until death us do part."

"This is my solemn vow."

Abram smiled so big Robin wondered if his face would crack. He turned to Tony. "Will you, Antonio, take this woman, Robin, to be your beloved bride? Will you love and cherish her, protect and provide for her, in good times and in bad, in times of failure and in times of triumph, for better or for worse, for richer, for poorer, in sickness and in health, and—forsaking all others—remain true and faithful to her for as long as you both shall live?"

Tony squeezed Robin's hand. "I will."

"Then in the presence of God and all those gathered here, repeat this solemn vow which you will uphold from this day forward," Abram said. "I, Tony, promise you, Robin, that I will give you my heart and my life."

Tony spoke the words clearly, his strong voice ringing through the church. As he repeated the vows he had written for her and with her, she felt tears burning her eyes and furiously blinked them back afraid makeup would run if she let them fall. Every sentence he spoke, she fell more and more in love with him.

"I will stand by your side in sorrow or in joy."

"I will care for you and protect you."

"I will support you in all that you do."

"I will laugh with you and cry with you."

"Above all, I will love and cherish you as your adoring husband until death us do part."

"This is my solemn vow."

The look on his face was intense, making her believe him, telling her that he would treasure her love.

Abram said, "May I have the rings?"

Barry and Maxine both stepped forward to release the rings off of Isaac's pillow. She handed Abram Robin's ring, and Barry handed Abram Tony's ring. As soon as he was released from ring duty, Isaac dropped his pillow and ran to the front row where his oldest brother sat. Robin could see Peter roll his eyes as a thousand people chuckled.

Abram laughed and then said, "Robin, place the ring upon Tony's finger and repeat after me."

Robin took the ring from Abram and mimicking her moves from the night before, placed it on Tony's finger and said, "With this ring I thee wed."

Abram nodded and said, "Tony, place the ring upon Robin's finger and repeat after me."

Tony gently held her hand and slid the band of sapphires and diamonds onto her left finger. He looked into her eyes and said, "With this ring I thee wed." Just for her benefit, he whispered, "Again."

Robin laughed. Abram paused and nodded, and a man and woman took the stage, getting the microphones from the appropriate place and moving to stand in front of the audience. When they started singing, "When God Made You," Tony and Robin walked hand in hand to a table that had two lit candles and a third unlit. They each took a candle, and together lit the third one, then extinguished the original two, symbolizing the coming together as one.

They moved back to their positions in front of Abram. As the song ended, he said, "By the power vested in me by the Creator of marriage and the church of God, and in accordance with the laws of the state of Massachusetts and these United States, I now pronounce you husband and wife. What God has joined together, let no one put asunder. You may now kiss your bride."

Tony stepped closer and put his hands on her shoulders. When his lips met hers, the audience around them faded away and she felt a warmth flood her body straight through her heart. She put a hand on the back of his neck and willed him closer even as he pulled back. He smiled and lifted her left hand, kissing her knuckles right above her rings. She reached for her bouquet from Maxine, then she and Tony turned around, hand in hand, and faced the congregation. For the first time, Robin looked around and saw every seat full, even in the upper balcony. She squeezed Tony's hand harder, and he laced her fingers with his.

Abram said, "Ladies and gentlemen, allow me to introduce to you for the first time ever, Mr. and Mrs. Antonio Viscolli."

THE END

TRANSLATION KEY

Buon San Valentino—happy St. Valentine's day
capisci—understand, comprehend
cara—dear (darling, beloved)
cara mia—my dear
figlio—son (esp. beloved male child)
Lei parla Italiano—Do you speak Italian
magnifica—magnificent
mio fratello—my brother
mia moglie—my wife
Napoli—Naples, Italy
non ne parlano—don't speak it (don't mention it)
qualunque—any
sì—yes
spiegati—explain
Ti amo con tutto il cuore e con tutta l'anima—I love you with all of my heart and soul
Touché—(French) touch. In dueling, it is a term that signifies an opponent has drawn blood with the tip of the foil.

DISCUSSION QUESTIONS

Suggested group discussion questions for *Greater Than Rubies*.

When asking ourselves how important the truth is to our Creator, we can look to the reason Jesus said he was born. In the book of John 18:37, Jesus explains that for this reason He was born and for this reason He came into the world. The reason? To testify to the truth.

In bringing those He ministered to into an understanding of the truth, Our Lord used fiction in the form of parables to illustrate very real truths. In the same way, we can minister to one another by the use of fictional characters and situations to help us to reach logical, valid, cogent, and very sound conclusions about our real lives here on earth.

While the characters and situations in The Jewel Series are fictional, I pray that these extended parables can help readers come to a better understanding of truth. Please prayerfully consider the questions that follow, consult scripture, and pray upon your conclusions. May the Lord of the universe richly bless you.

Tony felt led by the Holy Spirit to help Derrick DiNunzio. He followed through with that guidance and opened his home up to him.

1. What was your reaction to Tony's willingness to heed the call of the Holy Spirit?

2. How often do we as Christians ignore the need of at risk youth in our cities?

3. What can we as Christians do to help more at risk youth?

Jacqueline Anderson took Robin shopping to teach her how to adorn herself "more suitably" as Tony Viscolli's wife.

4. Do you agree that appearance is important? How important or unimportant is one's appearance when you are evaluating his or her character or intentions? How do you think your appearance may influence those around you positively or negatively?

Tony uses a board game as an allegory for life on this earth when he witnesses to Derrick.

5. Did Tony's illustration with the Monopoly board in any way change your perception of material possessions?

Tony is willing to get rid of his vast fortune in order to keep Robin by his side. Read Luke 18:18-23.

    6. Do you think Tony would have really given up "everything" to be with Robin?

    7. Christ has likened His relationship with the church as a marriage. What would you be willing to give up to follow Christ?

Read Abram Rabinovich's sermon during Robin and Tony's wedding ceremony.

    8. Do you agree with Abram's definition of marriage?

    9. What do you think it means to "give up oneself" for your spouse?

LUNCHEON MENU

uggested **luncheon menu for** a group discussion about ***Greater Than Rubies.***

Those who follow my Hallee the Homemaker website know that one thing I am passionate about in life is selecting, cooking, and savoring good whole real food. A special luncheon just goes hand in hand with hospitality and ministry.

For those planning a discussion group surrounding these books, I offer some humble suggestions to help your special luncheon talk come off as a success. Quick as you like, you can whip up an appetizer, salad, entree and dessert that is sure to please and certain to enhance your discussion and time of friendship and fellowship.

The Appetizer:

Sarah's Choice Falafel

Sarah's choices at a wedding may sometimes be limited. But, Robin knows what her sister will and won't eat, and this Falafel prepared by Viscolli's chef is a perfect appetizer.

INGREDIENTS

FOR THE FALAFEL:
1 pound (about 2 cups) dry chickpeas/garbanzo beans
1 small onion, roughly chopped
$1/4$ cup chopped fresh parsley
4 cloves garlic
$1 1/2$ tbsp flour
$1 3/4$ tsp salt
2 tsp cumin
1 tsp ground coriander
$1/4$ tsp black pepper
$1/4$ tsp cayenne pepper
Pinch of ground cardamom
Grapeseed oil for frying

FOR THE YOGURT SAUCE:
1 cup plain Greek yogurt
$1/2$ TBS lemon zest
1 TBS freshly squeezed lemon juice
1 TBS chopped cilantro leaves
2 tsp chopped parsley leaves
$1/2$ teaspoon ground cumin
salt, as needed (Kosher or sea salt is best)

PREPARATION

Cover the chickpeas with cold water and let them soak overnight. They will double in size to about 4-5 cups of beans.

Chop the onion.
Chop the parsley (divided) and cilantro
Zest and squeeze the lemon.

✥ DIRECTIONS ✥

Mix the ingredients for the yogurt sauce and refrigerate.

Drain and rinse the chickpeas well. Pour them into a food processor along with the chopped onion, garlic cloves, parsley, flour, salt, cumin, ground coriander, black pepper, cayenne pepper, and cardamom.

Pulse all ingredients together until a rough, coarse meal forms. Scrape the sides of the processor periodically and push the mixture down the sides. Process till the mixture is still textured but going toward a paste. (You don't want to over mix).

Transfer to a bowl. Cover and refrigerate for 2 hours.

Fill a deep skillet with 1 1/2 inches grapeseed oil. Heat over medium heat. While the oil heats, take 2 TBS of the falafel mixture and form it into a slightly squished ball. (The balls may not stick perfectly together as you're forming them, but they will bind together once you start frying.)

Gently place the balls into the oil, a few at a time, and fry for 3 minutes. Using a slotted spoon, gently turn them over and fry for another 3 minutes. Remove from oil and drain on a paper towel.

Serve with the yogurt sauce.

The Vegetable:

Cauliflower Mashed Potatoes with Asparagus

Nothing beats a creamy cauliflower mashed potato, and the steamed asparagus pair perfectly with the Rosemary Garlic Lamb served at Robin and Tony's wedding.

INGREDIENTS

15 red skinned potatoes
1 large cauliflower head
$1/4$ cup butter
$1/4$ cup half and half
$1 1/2$ tsp salt (divided) (Kosher or sea salt is best)
$1/4$ tsp fresh ground black pepper
2 asparagus stems per person

PREPARATION

Scrub the potatoes. Cut into chunks.
Break the cauliflower into small chunks

DIRECTIONS

Place the potatoes in a pot of cold water. Add 1 tsp salt. Bring to a boil.

Place the cauliflower in a steamer basket and place into the pot with the potatoes so that it can steam while the potatoes cook.

Cook the potatoes until a fork inserts into them easily.

Drain and transfer the potatoes and cauliflower to a bowl and mash (or us a potato ricer). Stir in the butter, cream, salt, and pepper.

While you're mashing the potatoes and cauliflower, steam the asparagus for 5 minutes.

Serve the cauliflower mashed potatoes with two pieces of asparagus draped over them.

The Entree:

Rosemary Garlic Lamb Chops

The Boston Viscolli Hotel is well known for 5-star international cuisine. Robin went with one of their specialties, rosemary garlic lamb, for her wedding banquet.

ℐNGREDIENTS

Lamb Loin Chops—2 per person
extra virgin olive oil—about 1 TBS chops
1 clove of garlic per 2 chops
1 sprig of rosemary per 2 chops
salt to taste (Kosher or sea salt is best)
fresh ground pepper to taste

ℐREPARATION

Mince the garlic.
Remove the rosemary leaves from the stems and chop the leaves.

ℱIRECTIONS

Lightly spray or using your finger, wipe, olive oil on the chops.
Rub the garlic and rosemary onto the lamb. Salt and pepper to taste.
Cover and refrigerate for several hours.
Cook on a hot grill or a hot skillet for about 10 minutes per side for medium to medium rare lamb. If you want it

done a little more, cook it to your taste.

The Dessert:

Heavenly Chocolate Covered Strawberries

Robin and Tony give their wedding guests the gift of chocolate covered strawberries decorated to look like wedding gowns and tuxedos.

INGREDIENTS

1 pound ripe, organic strawberries with stems
6 ounces dark chocolate
3 ounces white chocolate

PREPARATION

Chop the dark chocolate and the white chocolate separately.

DIRECTIONS

Melt both the dark and the white chocolate (separately) completely in a double broiler.

Dip the strawberries into the dark chocolate. Lift and twist, letting the excess chocolate drip off. Carefully set on parchment paper.

Dip a fork into the white chocolate and drizzle the dark chocolate covered strawberries.

Let chocolate set for about 30 minutes.

EXCERPT: EMERALD FIRE

Maxine **rolled over in** the bed. As the blankets slipped off, she felt cool air on her shoulders. While her partially asleep brain pondered that, she tugged the sheets back up to cover herself and her ring caught a thread on the blanket.

Her ring?

Maxine's eyes flew open as memories of the night before flooded her mind. She whipped her head around and stared at the empty space in the bed next to her, the pillow indented from where her husband's head had lain.

Her husband!

Alone in the bedroom, she lifted her left hand and stared. There sat the ridiculously enormous, preposterously expensive platinum ring, encrusted with emeralds and diamonds, that the man with whom she had been engaged for less than two hours before their wedding ceremony had picked out for her. When he slipped it onto her finger, he'd said something about the color of her eyes. Seconds later, he'd kissed her.

After a cursory glance around the room to be certain she was actually alone and the bedroom door was shut, she threw off the covers and rushed to the closet, looking for anything at all to wear. She grabbed a pair of jeans and a sweater and dashed to the bathroom, shutting and locking the door behind her. She leaned against the closed door for a moment while her heart raced and her mind reeled.

What in the name of all things holy had they done? Rather, what had she done?

With a few flicks of her wrist, she turned the water on for a shower and stopped to look at herself in the mirror. She lifted her fingers to her mouth and traced lips swollen from his kisses. Her green eyes sparkled like the stones on her hand. She normally had straight black hair and olive skin, both traits inherited from her father, a nameless one-night stand her mother would only ever crudely and often drunkenly refer to as Crazy Horse. But this morning her hair was mussed all around her head and her cheeks looked rosy, flushed. She felt warm inside despite the morning chill.

In her entire adult life, no other man had ever even so much as kissed her. Not once. Many men had tried to taste her mouth, but whenever they'd gotten close enough, panic would rise up and make her push them away. That typically ended the relationship. The ones who suffered that humiliation soon learned that it wasn't a one-time thing and very quickly gave up trying. As she stepped under the warm spray of water, she thought back to the night before and to her complete lack of fear.

Her husband of less than twelve hours—her husband didn't frighten her at all. When he kissed her, it occurred to her that she felt absolutely none of her normal panic. Instead, what she felt was warmth, excitement, attraction.

He made her feel safe. He made her feel... loved.

"Husband and wife," the Elvis impersonating officiator had proclaimed with a shimmy and a shake. Then her husband had slowly leaned in, leaned close, and taken her lips with his strong, masculine mouth as if her lips were the most delicate rose petals. Her knees had vanished and she felt his arm around her waist, holding her up, lifting her, supporting her as she kissed his heavenly mouth.

Then, here, in this hotel suite last night, her husband had carefully led the way. It was as if he sensed that she needed to be able to control the pace of the activity. She never had to say anything to him or explain her fear. He just accepted her hesitations or kissed her through them. He slowly coaxed and guided and offered until she accepted. It had been so wonderful, so beautiful, that he had held her to him with her head cradled against his broad, thick chest and his strong arms around her while she wept at the beauty of it.

Her sister, Robin, was going to kill her. Reflecting on that for a moment, Maxine realized she didn't much care. She was excited, thrilled. Married!

She quickly finished showering and got dressed. After brushing her teeth and running a comb through her hair, she left the bathroom, again comforted by the solitude. Little nervous butterflies woke up in her stomach while she slipped into her shoes, the sight of the enormous ring on her finger distracting her with every motion of her hand.

Stalling, she straightened the bed. As she pulled the coverlet up, her ring caught the light. Running her hand over his pillow, she smiled and felt a warm rush of love flow through her heart, quelling the nervous butterflies.

When she could think of nothing else to do, she opened the bedroom door and stepped out into the living room. Seeing him standing there staring out into the sunrise brought back visions of every time she had seen his face in the last three years. She thought of every time she had sketched his face. She could not believe how much had happened in the last three weeks.

The thought stopped her. Three weeks? Had it only been that long since they put her brand new husband's first wife in the ground?

He turned as soon as she opened the door and their eyes met across the room. Maxine's smile froze at the stoic look on his face. "Hi." His voice sounded low, scratchy, thick. She wondered if he had slept at all.

"Hi." She smiled. She noticed the cup in his hand. "Is there coffee, too, or just tea?"

Using the cup, he gestured at the room service cart sitting next to the table and chairs. "I didn't know how to make the coffee, so I just ordered you some instead."

Warmth flooded her heart at his thoughtfulness. "Thank you." She crossed the room and poured herself a cup. Her hand shook a little bit. What did they do now? What did they talk about? How did she handle this first full day of being a wife? His wife? More than anything at all, she wanted to please him.

When she turned back around, she saw that he had silently moved and now stood next to the couch.

"Obviously, we need to talk."

She didn't like the sound of his voice. No warmth, nothing she had felt from him the night before existed in his tone. She gripped the cup so hard she was surprised it didn't break. "Yeah." Needing to ease her own tension, she teased, "Kind of a little late for that, isn't it?"

The Jewel Series
by Hallee Bridgeman

Book 1: *Sapphire Ice*, a novel

Book 2: *Greater Than Rubies*, a novella

Book 3: *Emerald Fire*, a novel

Book 4: *Topaz Heat*, a novel

Book 5: *Christmas Diamond*, a novella

Book 6: *Christmas Star Sapphire*, a novella

Available as eBook or paperback wherever fine books are sold.

FICTION BOOKS BY HALLEE
Find the latest information and connect with Hallee
at her website: www.halleebridgeman.com

The Virtues and Valor series:
Book 1: Temperance's Trial
Book 2: Homeland's Hope
Book 3: Charity's Code
Book 4: A Parcel for Prudence
Book 5: Grace's Ground War
Book 6: Mission of Mercy
Book 7: Flight of Faith
Book 8: Valor's Vigil

The Song of Suspense Series:
Book 1: A Melody for James
Book 2: An Aria for Nick
Book 3: A Carol for Kent
Book 4: A Harmony for Steve

Standalone Suspense:
On The Ropes

PARODY COOKBOOKS BY HALLEE
Vol 1: Fifty Shades of Gravy, a Christian gets Saucy!
Vol 2: The Walking Bread, the Bread Will Rise
Vol 3: Iron Skillet Man, the Stark Truth about Pepper and Pots
Vol 4: Hallee Crockpotter & the Chamber of Sacred Ingredients

With more than half a million sales and more than 20 books in print, Hallee Bridgeman is a best-selling Christian author who writes romance and action-packed romantic suspense focusing on realistic characters who face real world problems. Her work has been described as everything from refreshingly realistic to heart-stopping exciting and edgy.

A prolific writer, when she's not penning novels, you will find her in the kitchen, which she considers the "heart of the home." Her passion for cooking spurred her to launch a whole food, real food "Parody" cookbook series. In addition to nutritious, Biblically grounded recipes, readers will find that each cookbook also confronts some controversial aspect of secular pop culture.

Hallee loves coffee, campy action movies, and regular date nights with her husband. Above all else, she loves God with all of her heart, soul, mind, and strength; has been redeemed by the blood of Christ; and relies on the presence of the Holy Spirit to guide her. She prays her work here on earth is a blessing to you and would love to hear from you.

You can reach Hallee via the CONTACT link on her website or send an email to hallee@halleebridgeman.com.

Newsletter Sign Up: tinyurl.com/HalleeNews/
Author Site: www.halleebridgeman.com
Facebook: www.facebook.com/pages/Hallee-Bridgeman/192799110825012
Twitter: twitter.com/halleeb

Hallee News Letter
http://tinyurl.com/HalleeNews/

Sign up for Hallee's monthly newsletter! Every newsletter recipient is automatically entered into a monthly giveaway! The real prize is you will never miss updates about upcoming releases, book signings, appearances, or other events.

Printed in Great Britain
by Amazon